Charmed Against All Odds

Secrets of Roseville • Book 5

Betty Bolté

Betty Bolté
www.bettybolte.com

Acknowledgments

My heartfelt thanks to my beta readers—
Danielle Bolté, Jennifer Carabello, Mandy Oaks,
and Rachel Capps—for their helpful feedback
on some of the finer details of the story.

Also by Betty Bolté

Becoming Lady Washington: A Novel
Notes of Love and War

FURY FALLS INN
The Haunting of Fury Falls Inn
Under Lock and Key
Desperate Reflections

SECRETS OF ROSEVILLE
Undying Love
Haunted Melody
The Touchstone of Raven Hollow
Veiled Visions of Love
Charmed Against All Odds

A MORE PERFECT UNION
Elizabeth's Hope
Emily's Vow
Amy's Choice
Samantha's Secret
Evelyn's Promise

Chapter One

A mere flick of her wrist. A clear and intent thought. A snap of her fingers. Any would do. Roxie Golden tapped the cluttered counter with her red painted nails. But it wouldn't be the right thing to do. She couldn't live with herself if she gave in to the weakness of temptation and used her magic for personal gain or benefit. She'd seen the devastating aftermath of such a selfish act. She shuddered at the vivid memory. No, better to endure the day-by-day efforts to put on the perfect wedding for her sister, Beth, and her fiancé, Mitch.

"You should write it." Tara, Roxie's youngest sister, peered at Roxie with hopeful, hazel eyes. Her long, chestnut hair fell in a braided rope over one shoulder. "You're the best with stringing together words with flare. It's your gift."

"You gals seem to be doing fine." Roxie would have rattled off exactly what played in her mind but didn't want to hurt her sisters' feelings.

Her animated and enthusiastic sisters had debated the wording for the wedding invitations for hours. Another wedding to plan. Yet for Roxie, a repeat of the old always-the-bridesmaid-never-the-bride syndrome. She mentally shrugged away the cynical inner voice. She didn't care if she never married since it couldn't be the man she had loved with all her heart. A once in a lifetime love. No amount of nagging and matchmaking by her sisters and cousins would change her mind let alone her devastated heart. She'd be glad when Beth married so she didn't have to suffer through another round of invitations, flowers, cakes, and all the other details. In the meantime, she'd grin and bear it. For the fourth and last time, now that her two cousins and her two sisters would all be safely wed.

"If you'd like, I can polish it after you're satisfied." She pressed her palm to the counter for a moment. "I'm sure you've laid down a strong start."

"Not good enough." Beth shook her head, making her shoulder-length, honey-blonde ponytail sway. "Please, Roxie, give it your mystical touch. I'm running out of time."

The Golden Owl Books and Brews store, the family business, was blissfully quiet for the moment. Roxie had much to do before the next rush of customers arrived. Boxes of books and coffee mugs designed for readers waited to be unpacked and put out for sale. Dusting of the rows upon rows of bookshelves on the second floor. Readying the stage for the evening's open mic night and the crowd that would descend on the store for wine and cheese as well as the poetry readings and musical performances. Ordering more donuts, pastries, and bagels for the coffee shop. She'd do whatever necessary to keep the shop running smoothly. Even tap into the customers' general feelings—though not their specific emotions which would be prying—when they browsed the offerings and then adapt the merchandise on hand to satisfy every need. Mother had passed on to a higher realm and left operations of the Golden Owl to her with her sisters' help.

Since Beth and Mitch would tie the knot in four weeks, Roxie counted the days until she could return to her normal, if humdrum, routine. If Beth's after-marriage attitude reflected Tara's after she'd wed Grant, then the bookstore management would fall squarely on Roxie's shoulders for the foreseeable future. Sure, her sisters showed up every day and puttered about. But both their minds were filled with thoughts about the wedding plans. Roxie shrugged mentally, acknowledging that Beth had every right to have the wedding of her dreams.

In the meantime, Roxie was forced to face the suggestive looks and unvoiced questions about her future. But only for another four weeks. Then everyone would carry on about their own business and forget her spinster status. The oldest sister unwed and even more unavailable.

Tara spun the sheet of notebook paper around, pushing aside a stack of bookmarks, a cup of mini red heart-capped pens, and a teetering stack of new release books on the jumbled counter, and handed the pencil to Roxie. "You're up."

"If you're sure…" Roxie glanced between their bobbing heads. The surge of inner joy and challenge made her heart pulse with a strong beat. She loved it when she was asked to help. "Fine. But go do something and let me think."

Everyone knew she possessed a unique way with language. Her spells had always been renowned among the Order for their flow and power. Her mother had said she was gifted with spell craft in addition to her innate powers. Not least of which was her ability to understand any language, including Mammal and Bird. She held her mother's compliment near and dear. But one thing she'd learned the hard way: better to let others lead and she would help from the background. Otherwise, they took affront.

Her fingers itched to reach for the ash wand she kept tucked in her waistband. Holding the slightly twisted wood helped to flow the magic through her body and mind. If only to assist with choosing the words to encourage family and friends to attend the joining of Beth and Mitch. They didn't know Mitch very well since he'd only arrived in town a few months before. But he'd quickly made himself a part of the family in spirit if not in fact. Once he and Beth married, they'd settle somewhere in Roseville and become more a part of the town. Folks just needed to give him a chance.

"We're going." Tara clasped Beth's upper arms and pushed her toward the back room. "We'll mosey on over to the laptop and start figuring out what flowers she wants in her bouquet."

"No roses, please." Beth grinned back at Roxie as she let Tara propel her into the work room where a mountain of boxes of books and merchandise waited to be put out on shelves and tables. "I want something unique and sturdy like me."

Roxie shooed away her laughing sister with a brief wave of one hand. "Very funny."

In fact, Beth embodied unique and sturdy after all her training she'd done over the past few months. Brazilian Jiu-Jitsu, yoga, firearms, and even a few flying lessons. Her personal skills had grown and transformed her into a woman with self-defense skills and the accompanying inner confidence.

"Thank you for appreciating my bit of humor." Beth chuckled as she disappeared into the room with Tara close behind.

Alone, Roxie studied the awkward attempt they'd made at wording the invitation to the wedding which would be held at the Twin Oaks Plantation Bed and Breakfast Inn. With the inn's ghosts laid to rest, thanks to the combined efforts of Roxie and her sisters as well as the inn's owners, the setting couldn't be lovelier for the ceremony and reception.

A distant flash of lightning outside the front window was followed seconds later by a low rumble announcing the approach of a storm. She glanced out to the busy street, noting with a vague sense of unease the dark gray clouds boiling above the low buildings of the typical southern town. She dropped her gaze back to the paper. After a couple of minutes, Roxie scribbled down a first draft of the invitation. She made several tweaks to the words and then tapped the pencil eraser against her lower lip. Other than the details of when and where, she wanted their friends and family to understand how Beth and Mitch felt about them.

"We invite you to witness our joyful union as the two people who fell in love and wish to spend the rest of our lives proving our love for one another. We hope all of our friends and family will agree to be part of our marriage and will join us in celebrating our new life together."

She added a line or two regarding the reception and then laid down the pencil when the musical bell over the front door jangled with a distinctly different sound. A wash of resistance flowed through her, an odd sensation. The summoning tones drew Beth and Tara out of the work room, curiosity etched on their features. Roxie looked to the door, still pondering the negative energy she sensed, then spotted a young man with dripping black hair and piercing tawny eyes. He hesitated before closing the door with a smooth, forceful thud. He seemed familiar but she couldn't place him. She squinted then blinked as she stared at him as his damp image clarified. Could it be? Shock ricocheted through her the longer she studied his stoic face. It couldn't be. But it was.

Leo.

He'd come back. Joy flooded her heart. Without further thought or consideration, she shrieked and ran across the store to bear hug her childhood sweetheart before planting a solid kiss on his astonished mouth. The contact revived the electrical current she'd always experienced when they'd kissed, a simmering sizzle flashing through veins. She pressed her lips to his, arms wrapped around his neck, for several seconds, relishing the taste of his mouth and the feel of his hard body beneath her hands.

She heard her sisters giggling behind her but didn't care.

Leo had come back. Finally.

She'd pushed his memory to the far reaches of her mind. The hurt when they'd broken off their engagement had lingered for years. A jolt of pain and longing went along with the many times she'd want to share a joke or insight with him. Wanted to share thoughts and impressions of her day. The visceral connection they once shared. His returning to Roseville dredged up the link from deep inside. An undeniable bond underlying every conversation, every activity, every moment they'd been together. Everyone, especially Roxie, had thought they made a perfect couple. Finally, she pushed back far enough to smile up into the familiar eyes.

"Leo. Welcome home." Roxie stared at him with delight which slowly wilted the longer she searched his surprised and defensive expression.

He'd changed since he'd left town. Taller and stronger, understandably since he'd been eighteen when he'd headed off to college six years ago. No longer the gangly youth but a fully developed man. Even without his superpowers, he'd become a muscular, powerful being. His gaze held hers with a hint of challenge lurking in their depths. Clean-shaven except for a light mustache, his tempting lips flattened into a straight line. So he hadn't changed so very much after all. He still didn't want her.

To be fair, she'd known he'd leave. He'd made no secret of his desire to move away to the big city. Something she'd resented at the time but eventually came to terms with. Despite loving him with her whole heart, she hadn't been enough. The memory poked the sore spot lingering in her heart as she built a protective shell around herself. He didn't look pleased to see her at all. More like he'd rather be anywhere else than stand in the bookstore.

Rolling thunder sounded above the store as the heavens opened and rain cascaded onto the passing cars and pedestrians hunched under umbrellas or raincoats as they hurried down the sidewalk. Roxie pitied the folks caught in the storm but only for a moment. Her attention jerked back to the seething man in front of her. She peered at her one-time fiancé with sorrow in her heart. He'd returned but not willingly.

"I don't live in this town any longer, thank goodness." Leo swiped a hand through his hair, showering raindrops onto the floor. Then shoved his hands into his front jeans pockets and took a step away from her. "I'm not staying, either."

Ouch. "What are you doing here?" Besides opening old wounds. She hardened the shell, ready to deflect any barbs he might shoot her way. After all, they hadn't split up on the best of terms.

"My father died last month."

"I'm sorry. I hadn't heard he'd passed." Roxie glanced at her sisters where they worked behind the bakery counter, but obviously eavesdropped. They shook their heads at her to confirm they hadn't been informed of the highly respected man's passing either. Leo's bland expression told her a lot about his attitude, mainly he didn't want to engage with her. Then why had he strode through the door like he belonged? "What does that have to do with us?"

Leo reached into his windbreaker pocket. "He left a note saying to bring this to your mother. That she'd know what to do with it." A silver heart-shaped box lay on his palm with a folded gold paper taped to the top of the lid.

"Mom died three years ago." A surge of remembered grief at the sudden loss of her mother clogged her throat.

Her mother would have known exactly why Homer King had sent the box to her. They'd served together for decades as the Supreme Priest and Priestess of the Order of Witchery Lore, otherwise known as OWL. Her mother's collection of witchery lore proved legendary and was housed at the OWL headquarters outside of town. After her mother died, Roxie and her sisters had no further contact with the Order. Roxie, in particular, had put the large circle out of her mind because they reminded her of when she'd first met Leo, and she really didn't want to relive those wonderful memories when her heart ached for him. So she'd shut the door and locked it, then thrown away the key to those recollections.

Now he stood before her without even a kind word or hello. Her defenses rose higher.

Leo offered the box to Roxie but she shook her head. "I don't know what that is."

"Read the note." He pulled the note from the lid and handed it to her.

"Perhaps with your renowned prodigious understanding of language you'll glean more from it than I did."

She frowned at the sarcasm in his tone but studied the paper in her hand. Dated five years earlier. Before her mother had passed. Since it was indeed addressed to her mother, Homer must have forgotten about the box's existence. Otherwise, wouldn't he have changed the directions to Leo after Peggy's death? Homer had attended the funeral for her mother, so he knew Peggy had died. Yet the note remained addressed to her mother. An unsolvable mystery. The note read pretty much as Leo had summarized. "My dear son, in the event of my death, take this box, unopened, to Peggy Golden at the Golden Owl Books and Brews. She will know what to do. Love always. Dad."

Folding the note, she handed it back to Leo. "That wasn't much help. What do you mean to do next?"

"The sole reason I'm here is to give you this box." He plunked it down on the glass display case by the register, knocking a stack of postcards advertising the open mic night across the surface. "Done. I'm out of here."

Wait, she wanted to cry out as he glanced at her and then away. He couldn't leave. She had questions only he could answer. If he'd stay long enough to hear them. He pivoted on one heel and marched toward the door.

"Stop." She hurried to pick up the silver box and then hurried after him, holding it with both trembling hands. She caught up to him and momentarily laid a hand on his arm to detain his rapid departure, sensed the deep agitation inside him even as the familiar sizzle flowed through her. She stifled a gasp. He glanced at her hand and then met her eyes with a steady look. Releasing his arm, she gripped the box with both hands. "What am I supposed to do with it?"

The box vibrated in her hands and then a lyrical click sounded as the lid popped open. What had unlocked the box? She blinked at it, angling it one way and another to search for a release or some other catch she might have brushed. Nothing. Tara and Beth came around the counter and stood to one side, peeking at the tiny box. Magic must have been infused in the object, sensitive to her touch. But only after she'd touched Leo. Before then, it had remained firmly secured. She stared at the box as if it held a secret she didn't want to know.

"Open it all the way." Beth stretched a hand toward the box but hesitated to make contact with it. "What's inside?"

"No idea. Not sure I want to but… Here goes." Roxie slowly lifted the lid to reveal another gold folded note under a chunky golden bracelet. A single charm—an open book— was attached to it.

Odd to have only one charm on a charm bracelet. She lifted the chain to inspect the little book. On the back of the gold charm the number thirty-three had been engraved. Frowning, she looked up into Leo's carefully schooled expression of disinterest.

"What on earth does it mean?" Roxie studied his strong, perhaps even beautiful, features, recalling how years before he'd been far more animated and attentive. Not only had he changed physically over the years, he'd grown distant and judgmental. "Do you have any idea?"

"Why would I know?" He shoved his hands into his black jeans again. "I didn't even know there was a box until a few days ago."

His posture and attitude screamed he didn't care, but the flash of curiosity in his eyes belied his act. Did he know more than he was willing to say? Or being honest and as lost as she was? She reached out with her mind but only sensed his strong desire to walk out the door coupled with a growing amount of intrigue. Nothing to suggest he withheld information or answers.

Roxie tossed a glance at each of her sisters but received only perplexed shrugs in reply. "Then who the heck knows?"

The bell jangled as a young couple entered the store, interrupting the sleuthing session as the man folded a dripping umbrella and the pair started toward the sisters. Leo waited impatiently for the distraction to be handled. He had better things to do than stand in the store, with Roxie. He'd hoped to avoid meeting her. He should have known better.

His lips still tingled from the sudden rush and press of the woman he'd once loved and expected to spend his life with. Once upon a time. Never again. Time changes things. He pressed his lips together, trying to calm the lingering sparks dancing across them. He clutched the desperation to return to his normal life like an invisible shield against her allure. Most things change with time, but apparently not the fireworks of Roxie's kiss. Nor the undercurrent of attraction threatening to unmoor him and carry him across the room to embrace her. Neither could happen.

Tara strode over to greet the chatty couple and then led them away toward the back of the store and the mystery section. Beth moved to greet the next customer into the store, a middle-aged woman with salt-and-pepper hair and a smile he thought might be a permanent fixture.

Merely standing in the bookstore flooded Leo's mind with fond memories of hours spent sitting in a chair in a cozy nook reading while Roxie worked. Hours of simply being near to his girl. She'd stop by and check on him, bring him a Coke and a kiss, then be off to help a customer select a book. He tensed as he brushed aside the memories. The past must not repeat itself. He couldn't stand going through that again.

He dragged his attention back to the matter at hand. He'd always loved a good puzzle, and the charm piqued his interest in a way he hadn't experienced in years. Maybe even since he'd left town. He'd been far more interested in proving he could succeed as a pitcher in the major leagues than solving mysterious clues. But this one fell into his lap and he couldn't ignore it.

"Thirty-three could mean anything. Wait…isn't it the age of Jesus when he was crucified?" Leo pinned his gaze on Roxie, who fingered the charm with her thumb and forefinger. "Maybe the book charm represents the Bible and a specific chapter and verse?"

"Mom wasn't overly religious, but it's a place to start. Come on." She closed the lid on the bracelet and hurried to the shelf of Bibles and related texts.

Her hand landed on a white bound book which she pulled off the shelf and flipped to the referenced page number, then checked several books and chapters of the same number. Scanning the contents, she frowned and then finally shook her head. She aimed beautiful, puzzled gray-brown eyes at him. "How would we know from reading all of these verses which one is linked to the charm?"

Resisting the urge to lean closer to peer at the page, determined to keep his distance, he shrugged instead. "Nothing stands out as insightful or instructive?"

She shook her head, long brown hair winking with gold brushed her shoulders, tempting his fingers. Snapping the book closed, she shelved it in one smooth motion and tilted her head to stare at him. "Since it's a book, which makes perfect sense, then it must be one that is meaningful. But to your dad or my mom?"

Their parents had worked closely to manage the volumes and tomes in the OWL archives. Running the immense library of witchcraft and magic documentation swallowed much of their time. Leo couldn't remember a period when he didn't know Roxie, as they'd grown up together. Not until junior high had their friendship morphed into something more. By high school they were dating each other exclusively and spent all their free moments together. He'd proposed their senior year and she'd leaped into his arms to accept. He'd thought they'd have a wonderful life.

Until she'd lowered the boom on any hopes of making such a plan happen. She blamed him for the breakup. Wouldn't even consider his side of the equation. His reasons for his actions. He'd moved away and moved on. Her attitude, shifting from the surprising kiss to acting all standoffish toward him, indicated she'd done the same and didn't appreciate him showing up out of the blue. He glanced to the rain falling outside. Make that, out of the wet.

"Your dad had the box with the charm. So I'd imagine it's his." She frowned at him.

"We don't know that. It could mean anything. But what does seem most likely is that it's a page number in some book or another." He rubbed his jaw, noting the beginning of stubble rasping across his calloused hand. "Since Dad sent it to your mom, I'd say it's probably something of hers. A cookbook? Or did she keep a diary?"

"She didn't use recipes." Roxie wrapped her arms around her waist and regarded him with serious eyes. "I don't think she journaled either. Not that I ever saw."

Just then the door opened and a tall man strode into the store, raindrops glistening on the shoulders of his black overcoat. Leo figured the man to be an athlete, with the loose, powerful stride, and the friendly blue eyes weighing him as he approached. Roxie hurried to the front of the store and gave him a hug. Leo trailed after her in a slow saunter, hoping to learn more about who the stranger was to her. Not that he was jealous. Just curious.

Roxie turned to address Leo as he stopped beside her. "Leo, this is Max Chandler. He is not only a conservation lawyer but he also married my cousin, Meredith, and lives with her out at Twin Oaks. Max, Leo King is an old friend who's popped into town unexpectedly." She winked at Max with a slow smile, glancing between Leo and him. "With a magical mystery."

"I don't want to know about it." Max chuckled as he extended his hand to Leo and they shook. "Nice to meet you. I only came in for my morning java and to see if maybe you found my keys. No mysteries and no magic, please."

"Tara's working on your coffee now. What keys?" Roxie grinned at Max and then scanned the store.

"My office keys. I seem to have left them somewhere."

"That would be a problem if you can't get into your office." Roxie gestured to the coffee shop part of the store. "Have a look and see if they're on the counter."

"I will. How are things going with you?" Max shifted his weight to one hip, alert and observant.

The man glanced at Leo and then Roxie, giving Leo the distinct feeling he was being judged and found lacking in some important respect. Not the first time he'd endured such an evaluation. Vivid memories of how he'd deeply disappointed his father six years ago scrolled past his mind's eye. He fisted his hands in his pockets, refusing to let his own insecurities show.

"We've been quiet this morning." Roxie made a production of presenting the charm bracelet to Max, the lone charm glinting in the overhead lighting. "Which is good since it gives us time to figure out what this means."

"Thirty-three, huh?" Max stopped the slowly spinning charm with a blunt fingertip. "What's that mean?"

"That's the thirty-three thousand dollar question." Roxie sniffed and then huffed as she laid the bracelet back in the box. "An open book with a number. Probably a page number. But which book?"

"Whose charm is it?" Max slipped his hands into the back pockets of his blue jeans.

Roxie grimaced and shook her head. "Maybe my mother's. Leo found the box and note in his father's things when he came back to handle his estate."

Max looked more closely at Leo. "Your father was Homer King? I'm sorry to hear of his passing. He was a good man if a bit mysterious in his own right."

"Thank you. He could be rather uncanny at times." Leo didn't ask how the lawyer knew his father because it didn't surprise him.

Everyone knew his dad. Homer frequented the bars, the churches, the festivals so numerous in town. An active member of the Rotary Club, the Lions, the Chamber of Commerce, and even volunteered at the youth club on occasion. Homer King made it his business to know everyone else's, but kept his own business a closely guarded secret. Leo hadn't been aware of how extensive his business holdings and investments were until he'd started poking into his accounts and realized the magnitude of the job of executor.

"Which doesn't help us solve our mystery." Roxie set the box on the counter and crossed her arms. "So now what?"

"Think outside the box, I guess." Max shrugged as he considered the small group surrounding him. "Maybe it refers to the book on witchcraft your mother wrote. The one you recommended to Paulette last year when she was faced with gh…you know."

"Right. She needed help with sending Grandpa on his way. I gave her *Basic Witchcraft*. Be right back." Roxie rushed toward the work room, emerging moments later, flipping quickly through the pages of a small book. "I haven't looked inside this book in an owl's age… Aha." She lifted a folded piece of gold paper from between the pages.

"What's it say?" Leo sauntered toward her, resisting the pull of intrigue with each step. He couldn't allow simple curiosity to detain him in the small town he'd fled. His real life waited in Atlanta. Still the curiosity grew with each beat of his heart. "Read it out loud."

Roxie nodded and laid the book beside the silver box. She unfolded the paper and glanced at the bottom of the sheet. "It's from my mother."

My darling Roxie,

Years ago Homer and I realized how unique your friendship with Leo King would be. A powerful and everlasting bond if you'll only keep an open mind and heart. We're entrusting the two of you with a great gift.

Since you're reading this, my spell has been invoked. I'm assuming Leo has brought the jewelry box to you. Now you must work together *to collect all the charms designed for this bracelet in order to fully receive the gift we've created for you both. There are a total of 6 charms including the book. Each will lead to the next but you'll have to discover where they are located together. To find the next charm, solve this clue:*

Up and down and twist around,

Fast and slow we go

Up a hill and down a river
We've journeyed together.
What are we?

I know you two can do this. You have everything necessary. Once all of them are on the bracelet, read the spell I've left with the final charm and you'll have the answer to your most heartfelt questions and realize your true destinies. But I caution you, my dear. If at any time you stop working together, I've included a punishment to the spell which I hope you'll never experience. I do not wish harm to befall either of you, but it is imperative for you and Leo to complete the quest.

Trust me, my sweet daughter, and you'll find your forever happiness as well. Love you for eternity, Mom

"Oh my." Roxie stared at Leo as her eyes widened. "You know what this means, don't you?"

Leo's pulse throbbed in his neck as he waited with growing alarm the longer she glared at him. A buzz of dread inside his chest vibrated to his fingertips. "No. Should I?"

She drew in a deep breath and let it out slowly. "Mom has invoked a quest spell on us." She carefully folded the paper and slipped it inside the cover of the book. Then aimed her somber gaze on him. "Which means, my dear friend, that until we collect all of the charms you're stuck with me."

He put up both hands as if trying to stop a runaway train with just as much effect. "Hold on. I only came here to deliver that box. I'm not staying."

The very idea sent chills through him. Roseville held too few reasons to dawdle and yet too many fond memories. The combination repelled any chance of wanting to linger in the vicinity. Or to remain in proximity to Roxanna.

"But you have to." She shrugged, holding her shoulders by her ears for several seconds before lowering them. "We have to do this together."

"I only planned to be in town for a few days to get the ball rolling with Dad's estate." He slowly shook his head, denying any hint of the temptation to stay behind with her. He had his team to consider. His very job, for that matter. So late in the season, if he didn't return to take his spot on the roster and the mound, someone else would be happy to take his place. His personal trainer waited to up his workout regimen to help him move to the next stage in his fitness to boost his career. All waiting for him in the city. "This isn't part of my plan."

"Sorry, buddy. Your plans just changed." She rested one hand on a hip and arched both brows. "Until this quest is complete, you can't leave."

"You can't make me stay, either." Control slipped from his grasp with each passing second. He never should have followed his dad's quirky message. "I have to go home."

"You don't call Roseville your hometown anymore?"

"Not in years." He bristled at the umbrage in her voice. She had no right to chastise him for anything after the price he'd already paid. "This isn't home."

"Look, I know this is a surprise but it shouldn't take too long to figure this out. As long as we work together like Mom said, or rather actually insisted." Roxie considered him for a heartbeat and then sighed. "You going to stay at your dad's?"

"I can't. It's not officially mine yet." He'd started the legal process but until the will was probated the Order, as acting guardian of the property, couldn't turn over the keys to the house. "Even if it was, I couldn't sleep there. Not yet."

Roxie glanced across the open room at Beth and Tara working in the coffee shop, and then back to Leo, a slight frown dimming the light in her eyes. "I guess you can stay with me and Beth. No sense spending money on a motel."

Shocked into silence, Leo could only blink repeatedly as he tried to assimilate the sudden change to his agenda. He'd never once anticipated remaining in Roseville, not in a motel or at his dad's house. Then to be offered to stay at the Golden house? Of all the places in the universe. A shiver raced down his spine which he hid with a cough. Never. Not there.

"I don't know why you think I have to stay anywhere." He crossed his arms, the cold rain-soaked sleeves chilling him through, but he held his defensive stance. "Our parents are dead. They can't run our lives."

Roxie lifted one brow and slowly shook her head. "You've forgotten a lot, Leo. You know as well as I do how powerful our parents were. Not even death could break one of Mom's spells if she didn't want it to interfere. Whether you like it or not, you have no choice but to help me solve this quest. You're staying."

Leo straightened his shoulders, dropping his arms to fist his hands at his sides. "Maybe I see your point about the damn spell. But I'm not going to stay at your house."

"Fine. Stay at the B&B in town if you'd prefer. Just stay close."

Max cleared his throat, dragging Leo's thoughts back to the present. "Perhaps you'd be more comfortable out at Twin Oaks. It's a B&B and we have several openings. Meredith will even give you the family rate, I'm sure. You know, free… If you're interested?"

Sweet relief at another option trickled through him, thawing the shock into something less than a panicked response. Max seemed a decent kind of guy, gazing at him with understanding. Even without knowing exactly why Leo's resistance flared. He'd sleep in his car before he'd step foot in the Golden house again.

"I can't stay in this town any longer than necessary. My team needs me." Leo peered at Roxie, settling his wary gaze on her equally uneasy expression. She apparently didn't want him to stay either. Then why insist? "How long is this going to take?"

"I don't know but one thing is perfectly clear. Mom said not once but twice we have to work together to complete this quest. And she'll inflict some kind of punishment if we don't." Roxie stacked the silver box on top of the book and lifted them to hug against her chest. "The sooner we start, the sooner you can leave, as you wish."

The last shred of hope she'd forgiven him for his ill-advised transgressions flew out the window. Although they'd once upon a time been closer than he'd ever been with anyone else, she no longer felt the same way for him. If he still had his powers, he'd find out for himself her true thoughts about him. A quick dip into her mind to see for himself. Then he'd know whether she wanted him to pursue her or not. But her expression said enough. He didn't need his telepathy to read her face.

Misery snaked through his gut. She wanted him out of town as eagerly as he wanted to climb back into his hard-won sports car and drive away. The determination evident in her eyes and the prim set of her luscious lips showed she viewed the task before them as an unpleasant necessity. The truth in her mini lecture forced him to admit he couldn't win this particular argument.

"Lead me to Twin Oaks, Max." Leo heaved a sigh as he noticed Beth and Tara approach to stand by Roxie, the set of Max's lost keys dangling from Tara's raised fingers. "I guess I'm staying."

Chapter Two

The double parlor at Twin Oaks provided the neutral territory Roxie needed for the hastily called family meeting. With bowls of pretzels and mixed nuts on the end tables and various beverages in hand, her entire family clustered on the overstuffed chairs and brocaded loveseats surrounding the crackling fireplace. Waiting for her to clearly explain what she'd come to realize about the quest laid upon her and Leo's most definitely unwilling shoulders.

"My tea is cold." Paulette screwed up her face as she set her cup on the low table in front of her.

"So, go put it in the micro for a few seconds." Zak squeezed her shoulder with one large hand. "Lazy."

"Am not. I don't want to miss a thing." Wrinkling her nose, Paulette turned away from her husband to pin her hopeful gaze on Roxie. "Would you mind?"

"Of course not." Suppressing the bounding of glee inside, Roxie flourished her wand, aimed it at the flowered mug. She flicked the tip of the wand at the cup. Steam rose from the warmed liquid. "Try that."

Paulette lifted the mug and took a sip, aiming a grateful grin at her cousin. "Perfect."

Grant had one beefy arm around Tara as they sat on the loveseat facing the fireplace. His storm gray eyes held a hint of skepticism, the scientist in him still doubting his wife's abilities as well as her sisters. Despite having proof. Objective, irrefutable evidence and yet he continually showed that he doubted his own observation. Roxie pursed her lips as she studied the man. Ere long he'd have to acknowledge the abilities of the witch he'd married.

"What do you know about the quest spell, Roxie?" Beth sat on Mitch's lap in one of the chairs flanking the fireplace.

Mitch, too, tended to be reticent about the three sisters and their magical talents. Even though he would soon be a member of the family of witches with their individual gifts. Still, he'd only been part of the group for a couple of months. Over time, she hoped he'd come around fully to believe in them. Like Max and Zak.

"Enough to know that Leo and I may need all of you to help." She slid her gaze to take in the rest of the group.

Max and Zak had married the Golden sisters' cousins, Meredith and Paulette, respectively. The owners of the Twin Oaks plantation and B&B, the sisters had been instrumental in freeing the two ghosts who once haunted the place. Luckily, the ghosts were friendly and not scary. A whole different kind of magic might have been necessary in such a case. Roxie's wand fingers itched at the thought. It had been too long since she'd had a solid reason to seriously wield her wand. Warming her cousin's tea did not satisfy the itch. She put her wand away with a reluctant sigh.

Leo drew her eye as he paced like a caged panther, stalking from one end of the parlor to the other and back again. If he kept on, he'd wear a path in the antique oriental carpet. His quick glances at her said a lot about how much he resented being held in town. Well, she didn't want him in town against his will any more than he wanted to be. Best to begin in order to more quickly end.

All eyes watched her as she pressed her hands to her thighs and pushed to her feet before moving to stand in front of the fragrant fireplace, effectively cutting off Leo's path.

"Leo, sit down and let's talk." Roxie motioned to the chair she'd been sitting on.

"Talk, talk, talk." He hesitated, staring at her until she pointed more insistently. Frowning, he strode to the vacated chair and flopped into its depths, crossing his arms over his chest. "Get on with it, then."

His resentment flowed off of him in waves, nearly choking her. She blocked the stream of intense emotion while deciding on what she needed to convey to her audience. "I understand you're upset by all of this, Leo. My mother must have had strong reasons for setting up such an elaborate quest spell to bind us."

"What do you mean?" Grant shifted to lean forward, his thick brown hair glinting with red and gold strands in the firelight, elbows resting on his knees, to peer at Roxie.

"On the way here, I realized Mom must have believed there'd come a day when Leo would return to Roseville and…"

She hesitated to say the words out loud. Painful memories lurked at the edges of her mind, ones she'd tried but failed to banish. So many sweet moments she'd shared with the agitated man. So much love and laughter over so many years. All gone. Consumed by the closed off, reluctant, and antagonistic person staring at her with distrust. She clasped her trembling fingers together in front of her as she drew in a calming breath.

"And…what?" Meredith crossed her legs and then grasped her upper knee with both hands. "You can tell us anything. We're here for you."

"Thanks. It's hard to put in words." Roxie had liked Meredith since the first time they'd had an actual conversation.

Even before Paulette had finally discovered they were all cousins. Roxie's mother had revealed to the three sisters the relationship between the O'Connells and the Goldens long ago when they'd been discussing the family tree, going over it branch by branch. Only when Paulette had unearthed the fact that Roxie's mother, Peggy Jackson, had married Roscoe Golden, had the five women learned just how close the family ties were.

Roxie's gaze automatically went to the oil painting of her grandfather hanging on the wall. Her father, Roscoe, was the illegitimate son of her grandmother, Georgette Golden, and her grandfather, Patrick Finn O'Connell, a World War Two soldier and former ghostly visitor to Twin Oaks. Georgette never married and so her son retained her last name. If Paulette hadn't inadvertently summoned Papaw Finn, they may never have learned of their relationship. A revelation worth having despite having to deal with the prankster ghost.

"Roxie?" Meredith prodded with a querying raised brow.

"Right. Where was I?" Roxie sighed and shifted her gaze to rest solidly on her cousin. "I think she anticipated that Leo would eventually come back to Roseville…and to me."

"She couldn't know that." Leo straightened his back, gripping the armrests. "No way."

Roxie dragged her gaze to meet the surprise in Leo's. "Why else would she have emphasized the need to find all the charms together? She said if I had the box and bracelet then you must have returned. Somehow she knew you'd come back. To me." She carefully kept the stress even on the last word though her heart urged otherwise. She hushed her heart from adding "to us" as that might further push him away.

Leo sprang to his feet, fists on his hips. "This is ridiculous. I can't believe your mother would harbor such fantasies after what she did to me."

That long ago day, the last time Roxie laid eyes on the bristling man before her, her mother had done his father's bidding. Binding Leo's powers until he matured enough to use them wisely. Which ended up being forever now with both parents passed on. No other witch possessed the power to break her mother's spell. No one.

"And yet she apparently knew you'd come home." Roxie stepped in front of Leo to capture his attention. "She had her reasons. We have to do what she has laid out in order to understand what they are. *Together*, Leo."

Leo started to spin away, but Roxie grabbed his corded forearm and held tight. He lifted his gaze to glare at her. "I have to be back at work at the end of a week. The World Series is only a few weeks away so I cannot be gone longer than that and expect to still have a job. If the quest isn't done by then, it won't be. Got it?"

She could tell he balanced on a razor's edge before walking away and not looking back. Such an act would only lead to terrible consequences given the nature of the spell. She had to make him understand the risks involved with the spell, of the danger to them both should he run away from his obligations. Make him agree to follow the clues until the conclusion. She drew in a deep breath and squared her shoulders.

"Leo, we have to work as a team, as partners, because no one can break this spell except the completed charm bracelet. That's how a quest spell works." She squeezed his arm to keep his attention on her. "This is extremely serious. You cannot leave town until we've discovered all six charms and they're on the bracelet. Only then will we be free of the spell."

He jerked his arm free and shook his head. "What happens if we can't find all of them? Am I stuck in this place forever?"

"Mom wouldn't have made it impossible, but probably difficult." Physically or emotionally, or both? She sighed and splayed her hands. "As to what happens if you leave before we're done? She said she's applied some kind of safe guard that would evoke consequences in such an event. I don't want to find out what they might be. She was a very creative witch. There was a reason she'd made it all the way to the top of the Order of Witchery Lore as Supreme Priestess. Let's not find out what those protections or deterrents might be. Please?"

Max cleared his throat with a loud grunt, interrupting the tense moment, a frown clouding his normally crystal blue eyes into a soft gray. "The Order of…what did you call it? You've never spoken about an Order before. What exactly is that?"

Roxie could only stare at Max as his question registered in her shocked brain. She'd buried the existence of the Circle so far she hadn't even told the most recent additions to her family about them. Yet she'd grown up playing with the children of the witches who formed the dozen covens associated with the Order. The flow of ceremonies and rituals, of annual gatherings and those for special occasions and funerals, had underpinned her life. Until her mother died. Then everything had changed.

"The Order is the ultimate authority in this region." Leo pivoted to answer Max's question, a scowl marring his handsome features. "My dad and Peggy were the head honchos at the OWL headquarters for decades. They made the rules and exacted punishment on its members at their discretion."

Roxie shook her head with short, jerky movements. "They did more than that, but Leo is concerned only with their role as enforcers." Roxie drew in a long breath and let it out slowly. "See, Mom punished Leo for something he did in high school. Which is when he left."

When she had to find a new way to peace and happiness. She no longer had the love she and Leo once shared to sustain her. Looking back, she could see how she'd naturally turned to her sisters and her mother to fill the void he'd left in her heart. Tears pressed the corners of her eyes but she blinked them away. Blood love conquered all else.

"I remember." Tara pressed closer to Grant as she cut a glance at Leo. "Not a good day for anyone."

Beth clasped Mitch's hand, resting both on her thigh. "I'm sorry it came down to such drastic measures, Leo."

He inclined his head in acknowledgement of their sympathies. "I don't fault your mother so much as my father. It was his idea. No changing the past, especially now. But thanks."

Roxie studied his tense jaw and throbbing pulse in his neck. The very spot he loved for her to press a feather light kiss as they snuggled together on the porch swing. Whoa! Where did that memory come from? She had to rein in her thoughts and emotions and concentrate on the very real threat they faced.

Meredith raised a hand, wiggling her fingers to draw Roxie's gaze. "What does the Order do exactly?"

Glad for the direct question, Roxie addressed her cousin. "The Order houses an extensive library of all forms of media related to witchcraft. The study of the power of words and spells is the penultimate mission of the Order." Roxie glanced to each of the people in the room. "It was a natural next step for Mom to call the bookstore, with its offerings of related topics, the Golden Owl Books and Brews."

Zak jumped to his feet, sloshing the sweet tea out of his glass. "I get it now. I thought it had to do with the alchemist's journal but it is much broader than that."

Paulette grabbed a cocktail napkin from the end table and mopped up the fluid, then wadded the napkin and dropped it back on the table. "Careful next time, dear."

Leo's lips formed a small smile as he watched Zak's excitement. "Meaning?"

"The owl." Zak glanced around the room and then back to Leo. "You don't know the mythology?"

Roxie shook her head along with the others although she vaguely recalled something about them being related to magic. She should have known Zak, the chemist, would also be fully versed in mythology. "Enlighten us."

He bobbed his head and smiled. "When I first saw the store's sign, I thought it was tied to the symbolism of alchemy with the triangle being upside down and all. But the owl itself has served as a guardian of the underworlds and a protector of the dead in many ancient cultures. Native Americans revered it as the keeper of sacred and secret knowledge."

"Oh, that's right." Tara spoke up with bubbling excitement. "I remember Mom saying that during the medieval times owls were thought to be witches and wizards in disguise. I always thought it was amusing that she'd use the owl for the symbol and name of the store."

"I hadn't made the connection." Beth shifted on Mitch's lap as he pulled her back to lean against him. "Mom was way more clever than she let on, wasn't she?"

"That's one word for it." Leo dropped his shoulders into place as he grunted once. "I don't like being manipulated from the grave."

"Me, either. But we have no choice." Roxie pressed her lips together, contemplating the stoic stony expression on his face. "I can't do this alone."

Leo looked away, staring into the flickering orange and yellow flames for several ticks of the grandfather clock. Roxie stilled, uncertain of which way he'd go. Her heart beat oddly for several beats before settling into a normal rhythm. She studied the blank stare he aimed at the fire. Afraid he'd walk away and they'd find out just how clever the punishments from her mother's spell might be. Finally, Leo pinned her with a stern look.

"One week. We're not going to waste time on this. Deal?"

If that's all he'd commit to, then she'd take it. Better than nothing. Roxie stuck out her hand, hoping against hope seven days would be long enough. "Deal."

After a sleepless night at Twin Oaks, Leo waited impatiently for Roxie to make her appearance at Amber's Café. They'd agreed to meet and discuss the riddle over breakfast and map out their strategy. He gulped down lukewarm coffee and nearly spit it out. Flagging down the waitress, he asked for her to heat it up with some hot and then returned to watching the front door.

The discussion at Twin Oaks had prompted all kinds of memories of his high school years to resurface. He'd reveled in sports and the friendly competition, even when it grew heated. He loved to run and jump, so he played basketball for a year. Until he discovered baseball and the sheer delight of being out on the field under a deep blue sky and center stage on the pitcher's mound. Not that he craved attention so much as the sense of power it evoked to control the pace of the game based on the types of pitches he threw. How many walks, runs, and ultimately innings if the two teams were evenly matched and had to keep playing past the standard nine. He could run faster and move quicker than anyone else on his team. He gloried in his abilities which the others envied, as he could see in their open minds.

In fact, by his senior year, he had the distinct impression his dad feared his capabilities. His greater and growing strength, speed, and abilities with his mind. Even the new one he'd only begun to experiment with: telekinesis. Able to move solid objects by concentrating on a specific thing and its preferred location. Then he slipped up by using his mind control on the coach to secure a position on the varsity team then bragging about it to Roxie. Little miss play-by-the-rules

Roxanna had gone to her mother, who of course went to Leo's dad.

The rest of the story was old news.

He thanked the waitress for hot coffee and stared into its depths. Regret and disappointment brewing inside. What more was he capable of that he'd never experience because of one mistake? He'd gone on to be a successful, talented pitcher for the Braves, despite the binding of his powers. An accomplishment that gave him great pride since he'd done it on his own without relying on supernatural traits. But the whole debacle achieved one thing he never thought could happen. The shame forever changed how he felt about the one place—the school's baseball diamond—where he had thought he could be himself.

Finally, ten minutes later than agreed, Roxie pushed through the door. Dressed in blue jeans and a lightweight purple sweater, a crimson bag slung across her torso, she made her way the short distance to where he waited at a table. She'd pulled her long hair into a yellow clip at the back of her head. Both practical and alluring, allowing a glimpse of her delectably slender neck. He forcefully tamped down the memory of pressing his lips to the spot beneath her ear. No going back. That's not why he stayed. Her hazel eyes held cautious hope as she slid onto the seat across from him.

"Good morning. Did you sleep well?" She studied him for a moment and then waved down the waitress to request hot coffee. "I didn't."

"Good morning and I'm sorry. I didn't either, though." Leo gratefully swallowed the hot and full-bodied brew. "Thinking about that damn riddle all night hasn't helped."

Roxie stirred cream and sugar into her steaming mug. "Right? I feel more confused this morning about it than I did when I first read it."

She pulled the crimson cross-body bag around to the front. Reaching inside, she withdrew the silver box and placed it off to one side. Then delved back inside to retrieve the first clue, which she smoothed out on the table between her coffee and the box.

"Let's read it over again carefully and see if something jumps out at us." She chuckled and cast a wry smile at him. "Figuratively speaking, that is."

"Very punny." He rolled his hand at the gold paper. "Go for it."

"Here goes. First line is 'Up and down and twist around.' What do you think that might be?"

"I've thought and thought on that. Since your mother has insisted we work together, perhaps the clues have something to do with things we've done together?" He regarded her pretty features, striving with an effort to take care of the task at hand.

"That's a good point." She perused the words again and then met his gaze. "The next line is similar. 'Fast and slow we go.' I wonder if those lines refer to driving a car? Or riding on something?"

"Possibly." An inkling floated at the edge of his consciousness. "What's the next line?"

"The next two seem coupled. 'Up a hill and down a river, we've journeyed together.'" She contemplated him silently, taking a sip of her coffee and then setting down the mug. "Taken all together, I'm thinking of when we started hanging out together."

"'Up a hill'…up the roller coaster at the Valley Amusement Park?" Leo drummed the fingers of his right hand on the table. "'Down a river'…the flume ride?"

The waitress bustled over and poured hot brew into their cups but as she pulled the carafe away from Roxie's mug, she bumped the silver box. It crashed to the floor, opening and spilling the charm bracelet into the path of a family with several children hurrying behind the waitress. Roxie pushed back her chair and stood but too late. A young girl scooped up the shiny bauble with a cry of joy as the waitress sidled away. The girl bounced in front of her mother, holding up the gold bracelet to show her. Leo braced to intervene, but Roxie motioned for him to sit tight.

"What do you have, hon?" The mother gently extracted the bracelet from her daughter's clutches with a quick side glance at Roxie, who had stooped down to pick up the silver box. "Thanks for picking this pretty bracelet up for the nice lady. I'm sure she wants it back, don't you?"

The girl pouted and tears sprung to her eyes. "I found it."

"Yes, and it's a good idea to return it to its owner. Wouldn't you want someone to do the same for you? What if you lost Matilda? Wouldn't you want her back?" The young mother motioned to the rag doll tucked under her daughter's arm then kissed her on the head before turning to Roxie. She offered the bracelet to her. "Here you go. Have a blessed day."

Roxie nodded once and then squatted down in front of the girl, holding the bracelet safely in her hand. "Thank you. I don't know what I'd do without this. My mother gave it to me to remember her by now that she's gone to heaven."

"Welcome." The girl's lips trembled into a smile.

The mother took the girl's hand and led her toward the door where the father and brothers waited. Roxie waved to the little girl when she turned back to offer a shy wave of her hand. Then Roxie slid back onto her chair to resume her conversation with Leo.

"You need to be more careful." He clutched his mug with one hand. "What if you'd lost the bracelet? Then what would we do?"

"I'll guard it with my life." Roxie pressed her lips together for a long moment. Then shut the gold bracelet inside the silver box. She peered at him for a beat. "Now what were we talking about?"

"The amusement park." He hadn't thought about the

amusement park in years. On purpose. He'd pushed it so far down into the dungeon of his memories he couldn't recall clearly how long ago they'd first met. "When was that?"

She leaned back, her long fingers toying with the silver box. "We were ten. It was the annual Order gathering, bringing the families out to socialize. Mom told me she wanted me to meet you."

"Dad said something similar." A sudden thought flashed through his mind and then settled into place. Why had he never seen what their parents had been so clearly up to even when he and Roxie were children? Pushing them together subtly but insistently nonetheless. "Like they needed us to become friends or something?"

She nibbled on her lower lip as she slid her gaze away to take in the entire café. He let his own gaze drift after hers. Amber's proved a busy place on a Saturday morning. Chatting customers occupied half of the dozen tables in the bright dining area. Vases of red and pink flowers sat on each of the red vinyl table tops along with the salt and pepper shakers, blueberry and maple syrup pitchers, and a small sign advertising strawberry crepes with whipped cream topping. Two waitresses in pale blue skirts and white blouses hustled around refilling coffee or delivering a stack of steaming hot cakes. The mingling aromas of coffee, maple syrup, and fried bacon drifted past his nose.

"What are you thinking, Roxie?" His stomach growled and his gaze dropped to the menu on the corner of the table at his elbow. Looking back at her, he was surprised by the consternation in her expression. "What's wrong?"

"I think you may be right. They may have wanted us to be friends."

"What's wrong with that?"

She shrugged lightly as she opened the silver box. "Nothing. I'm glad they approved. We did have some fun together, didn't we?"

"We did." Leo craned his neck to read the upside down writing on the slip of paper. "What was the last line of the clue?"

"It says 'what are we?'" She stared at something over his shoulder, deep in thought. Suddenly, she blinked and smiled. "I know. It's what you said. Friends. That's what it's referring to. Where we became friends."

"Which was at the park." Leo smiled at her as the memories of their times together on the rides surfaced. They'd returned year after year to ride the roller coasters and tilt-a-whirl and many others. The house of mirrors had made them both laugh and the haunted galleon had made her scream and seek him out to protect her from the ghouls and wenches. Having her clinging to his arm for protection made him puff his chest out with pride. Back then. But not now. "Do you think the charm is hidden there?"

"Probably. After all, that's where they orchestrated us into becoming friends." She glanced at her cell phone display and grimaced. "It's not open yet, though."

"Let's have breakfast then and wait until they open the gates." He lifted his coffee and drank a long swallow. Then slid the menu in front of him, scanning the drool-worthy options.

"Sounds like a plan. I'm starving." Roxie fiddled with the silver box and then reached inside to lift the bracelet into the morning light. She caught his eye. "I think I'll wear the bracelet so it's always with me wherever I go. You never know when we might stumble upon the next charm and I don't want to be wondering where the bracelet is."

"Agreed. It's safer to have it on you." No little girls to steal it away even with the best of intentions. He held out a hand, palm open. "Want me to put it on for you?"

Now why had he asked such a thing? But the words had escaped, the offer hung suspended in the air between them. She'd most likely refuse.

Without a word, she laid the bracelet on his palm and held her hand out, waiting.

He fumbled with the clasp but finally opened it. Holding each end of the gold chain between thumb and forefinger of his hands, he wrapped it around her wrist. When he fastened the clasp, his fingers encountered delicate skin and a fine buzz traveled straight up his arms and into his soul. The gold seemed to glow briefly. He blinked and was relieved to see it had been his imagination. But his reaction to touching Roxie's skin hadn't been. He'd nearly forgotten the sensations he'd once felt for her. They'd become more than friends after they'd reached high school. So many years ago and much had changed in the interim. He pulled his hands away to pick up the menu again and study it, rather than look into her eyes and see what reaction she might have had to his inadvertent touch.

"Leo."

Slowly, somewhat reluctantly, he raised his gaze to meet her smile. "What?"

"Thank you for staying. The quest must be important or Mom wouldn't have created the spell." She picked up the box and the note and scooped them back into the crimson bag, zipping them safely inside. "Can I see the menu, too, please?"

Flustered, he nodded and laid it down so they could both see the options. "Sorry."

"We'll eat and then drive out to the park. It should be open by then." She perused the menu, trailing a finger down the list until her hand rested near to his.

He stared at her hand. So close. Remembered with vivid clarity the love they had shared. How would it feel to rediscover such an emotional bond with Roxana? His Roxie? To slide back to the warm, velvety place they shared? He blinked and looked away from her hand, moving his to grab his coffee cup and wiggle it at the passing waitress.

He couldn't do it. Couldn't pretend nothing had happened before but he couldn't relive that time either. His team needed him more than he needed anyone else. He had to see the end of the quest and then go back where he belonged. Away from his Roxie.

Chapter Three

The Corvette eased into the half-full parking lot as if Leo were afraid the gravel would hurt the vehicle. The spinning Ferris wheel brought a smile to Roxie's lips. Her all-time favorite carnival ride remained the tall wheel. A flash of an image from high school made her tense. She and Leo snuggled together in the center of the wide seat, stealing kisses as they reached the top and had a cherished moment of privacy. Out of sight of her sisters and their parents below. Gazing out over the twinkling lights from houses and farms surrounding the park, evidence of the residents living their lives. She couldn't walk down that memory lane. Better to change the subject and fast.

"Where could it be hidden?" She gestured to the acres of rides and games and show stages comprising the Valley Amusement Park. "I mean, there are so many possibilities and it's such a small thing."

"Worse than a needle in a haystack." Leo parked the car and prepared to step out into the late morning sunshine. "A pin head in a hayfield is more like it."

"Where do we start then?" Roxie followed Leo's lead and soon stood behind the sleek red car as he pressed the fob to lock the doors. "It could be literally anywhere."

Concern weighed on Roxie as she cast her worried eyes over the whirling, dipping, and climbing rides. The groups of laughing and yelling kids racing around from one ride to another, one game to the next. The sound of clarion music from the merry-go-round clashed with the twang from the blue grass band performing on the nearest stage, surrounded by avid listeners clapping along. How would they ever locate a tiny gold charm amongst so many places to hide one? If they didn't meet Leo's imposed deadline, couldn't locate the second let alone all of the remaining five charms, then what? The fear of that particular unknown made her hands tremble.

"How do you want to start?" Roxie interlocked her fingers to calm their movement. "Where do you want to start?"

"By paying admission so we can go inside and make a plan." Leo cut her a sideways look and then strode toward the entrance. "Let's get this over with."

She hurried to keep up with his longer strides, acutely aware they shared the desire to finish the quest as soon as possible. Without strolling down any memory lanes which might—who was she kidding?—*would* dredge up painful yet sweet memories of when they'd been an item. She struggled to shut and lock the door on those memories as she matched pace with Leo.

Inside the gates, they paused near a vendor's food wagon to scan the park map. The aroma of fried chicken tenders and French fries wafted past Roxie, making her mouth water while they pored over the park's layout. The tantalizing scent conjured a host of memories. Tenders and fries had been their traditional shared meal whenever they visited the amusement park. She'd fed him fries, one at a time. He'd sometimes put one end in his mouth and then she'd start nibbling from the other end, much like the spaghetti noodle in *Lady and the Tramp*. Ending with a laughing kiss in Leo and Roxie's case. She squelched the flush of desire, denying her reaction with every fiber of her being.

The park had expanded in the years since she'd last spent any time within its boundaries. A new waterslide and zip line stretched across the back third of the property. But the kiddie rides still clustered at the front left corner, and the big-kid rides took up most of the middle. Various music and theater stages stood in between the rides along with food vendors and games. Over everything the combination of sound and scent and flashing lights made for a merry and exciting atmosphere. She inhaled the pleasing aromas around her and then bit her lower lip. Should she suggest it? How big of a hurry might he be in? Only one way to find out.

"You want to grab some chicken and fries and a soda?" She pointed to where the vendor handed out paper plates with piles of fried tenders and fries to customers waiting in line. "I'm suddenly starving."

"Are you always hungry?" Leo folded the map and tucked it into his back pocket, a wry smile sliding onto his mouth. "We just finished breakfast, you know." He stared at her overdone pleading look and then shook his head. "Okay, fine. If we must."

"We must." Elated, she led the way over to the line of people. "After we eat, maybe a plan will spring to mind. I'm too hungry to think straight."

A small smile bloomed on his mouth. "You haven't changed. But you know, if your mother seriously laid this whole thing out years ago, it's highly likely someone else found the charm already."

"I hadn't thought of that." Her heart fell at the sudden fear of failure his words evoked. She shifted her weight to one hip as she considered the likelihood of the possibility. Shaking her head, she pressed her lips together as she peered at him. "I think Mom would have ensured only the two of us could locate and retrieve the charms. She'd have protected them with a spell of invisibility at the least."

"We still have hope of finding them if so." He took a couple of steps closer to the front of the line and then caught her eye. "Do you think she'd hide it someplace where we would have gone together back…"

When they were engaged. He stopped shy of saying the memory-invoking words but that didn't mean the memories didn't knock on the closed door. She ignored them. "Yes. Definitely fits her style."

Her cell phone played the opening refrain from "Devil with a Blue Dress On." "Hey, Beth. What's up?"

"Are you busy?" Beth's breathless voice made Roxie straighten from her casual stance.

"Not at the moment. What's going on?"

"Mitch and I can't agree on the wedding cake flavor. He's being obstinate about it being chocolate with caramel frosting, which is his favorite. I say we should go with a traditional white cake with the surprise taste of coconut frosting so it's all white and beautiful as well as delicious." A deep sigh followed. "What are we to do?"

"This is not a crisis, sis." Roxie moved closer to the front of the line when Leo stepped forward. "I'm sure you'll figure it out."

"I don't know…" Another long sigh. "Why is he digging in his heels on such a simple thing?"

"Why are you?" Roxie grinned and rolled her eyes at Leo. "Compromise. That's what you need."

The two of them had a tendency to think they each knew best. Wanted the other to fall in line with their opinion. Which would be fine except they couldn't do everything both ways. Some middle ground had to exist or they'd end up fighting over everything. After a while, the level of conflict would increase to the point they'd likely split up. An outcome Roxie intended to prevent at all costs. She simply needed to lend the proper tools to them to work out their differences and disagreements in a way to please both. If it came down to it, she might even say a few potent words of encouragement along such a path, but she hadn't needed to resort to weaving a spell for them. Yet...

"What do you have in mind? We can't afford two cakes, so that's not an option."

"Cupcakes?" Roxie imagined them alternating on tiered stands, icing swirled on top of each, with some white, some golden. "They'd look lovely and would give people choices as well."

"Love it. Thanks! I'll go tell Mitch." Beth chuckled over the phone. "Where are you? With Leo?"

"Valley Amusement Park and yes. We're about to grab lunch and then begin our search."

"Don't do anything I wouldn't." Beth laughed into the phone.

"Yeah. I've got to go." Roxie said her good-byes and slid her phone back into her pocket. No hanky-panky would be happening. Not today.

Leo ordered a large combo and added catsup to the paper plate. She grinned foolishly at him. He remembered. She dipped a fry into the red puddle. The first bite exploded in a delightful combination of sweet and salty flavors. She ignored the urge to offer him a fry, unwilling to go farther down the memory path. Before long they'd polished off the treat and thrown away their trash. The scene was too familiar to be ignored. They'd done the exact same ritual many times in the past. She looked at him expectantly.

"Can you use your magic to locate the charm?" He looked at her, all business, and then motioned to the busy scene surrounding them. "It might save us some time."

"I can try." She'd already determined they weren't there for anything other than to locate the charm. Why did she find his attitude upsetting, then? "Give me a minute."

She contemplated the right spell to locate a hidden magical item. She tugged him behind the vendor's stand where passersby wouldn't be inclined to notice her actions. Lifting her wand, she raised her other hand to the same height and then chanted the seeking spell. "Locatum spectrum mystism allum." A flick of her wrist and a burst of light spread outward from their position to encompass the entire park.

"Well?" Leo scanned the area and then contemplated her. "Anything?"

She searched with her powers and her eyes but found nothing. No inkling of a secret magical presence anywhere in the vicinity. "No luck. Maybe Mom anticipated I'd try to shortcut the process and guarded against using spells."

"Figures." Leo sighed long and loud. "Can't use magic to find magic."

"What now?"

"We need some kind of a plan." Leo scanned the vicinity, his gaze lighting on the tall wheel. "Want to get on the Ferris wheel and see if we can identify a likely spot?"

Keeping her eagerness carefully hidden, Roxie nodded. "We may as well." She kept her hands at her sides rather than reach to hold his as they made their way to the short line of people waiting for their turn.

"Could the charm be somewhere around here? We used to ride this together a lot." Roxie skimmed the surroundings, searching for any convenient places to stash the hidden charm.

Nothing stood out as a hidey-hole stable enough to have remained in one place for more than three years. The poles with their retractable bands for creating the snaking lanes for people waiting to ride wouldn't suit. The ride itself had a small hut nearby for the operator to shelter in from the weather, but one they couldn't access without raising eyebrows and questions she'd rather not answer. So likely not the right spot. Minutes later they took their seat on the ride and slowly swung backward and up to the top.

When they reached the very tiptop of the ride, the locked door in her mind sprung open. Unbid, a host of recollections rushed to the surface. She couldn't help the glance at him, noting the tense set of his jaw as he stared straight ahead. She turned away, not willing to stare at him, to force the issue of whether he recalled the sizzling kisses, the warm friendship of clasped hands as they strolled through the amusement park. His throwing a dart at the smallest balloon to win her the biggest prize, an oversized plush rainbow unicorn. Sharing the oh-so-sweet pink cotton candy and then kissing the sticky treat from his lips. Laughing at the stand-up comic at one of the stages. She steeled herself against sharing her thoughts with him as the wheel continued its revolutions.

Finally, the seat stopped at the bottom and she practically bolted from the ride before the bar had been fully lifted. She rushed down the metal ramp to the ground, dragging in deep breaths as if she'd had the wind knocked out of her. Searching the passing clusters of fun-seekers, her gaze was arrested by the steady stare of a middle-aged woman in flowered walking shorts and pink scooped-neck top standing under a shady tree. The woman pressed her right hand to her heart, the afternoon light glinting off of several rings on her fingers. Roxie used her enhanced vision to note the woman's wrinkled skin, faded green eyes, and steel-gray hair. But she focused more closely on the array of rings, spotting one on the woman's pinky she'd seen before. But the woman lowered her hand before Roxie could identify the stone. Then a surge of the crowd blocked her view for an instant and when they'd cleared the strange woman had vanished. All so quickly she might have imagined the entire episode. Only she knew with a deep certainty she hadn't. Roxie blinked as her brows dropped into a perplexed frown.

Leo stopped beside her and laid an arm over her shoulders, drawing her gaze up to meet his.

"You okay?" Worry shone from his eyes. "You look like you've seen a ghost."

Not a ghost, but someone she'd seen or maybe even met before. In a previous life or time? She shook off the sense of déjà vu. She'd meditate on the image later. "I'm fine."

"I don't believe you." He squeezed her shoulders and then dropped his arm to shove both hands into front pockets. "I don't think we're in the right place."

"Why?" She counted to ten, calming her agitation as best she could. Between the emotions stirred up by the ride and then the strange woman, she had to find her center in order to face what came next. "What did you recall?"

"Not so much a recollection as a feeling." He scanned the busy scene with all the people and noise and commotion. "Yes, we became friends here, but…"

"This isn't where we spent most of our time." She nodded as a thought formed. She mulled it over, inspecting the idea from every side. They may have spent time at the amusement park, but it wasn't where their friendship had been sealed. She stared at him, reluctant and yet resigned. "The store."

He glanced sharply at her and then grinned. "Let's go."

The drive from the amusement park to the historic Gordon's Drug Store flashed by. Leo's thoughts centered on the countless times they'd ridden their bikes to the landmark store on the outer edge of town to meet for ice cream. Fabulous homemade ice cream in dozens of flavors. Her favorite cherry chocolate chip and his butter pecan. His mouth watered at the very idea.

But he remembered so much more than simple pleasures. She'd made him laugh when she did impressions and screwy faces. He'd shared his essays and she'd helped him polish his prose, using her unique ability with languages. They'd shared their most private dreams, their loftiest life goals. Her desire to expand the bookstore's merchandise to include local artists and their talents. His goal to become a major league pitcher. In hindsight, conflicting goals but at the time they'd thought they could make it work. As long as they had each other. He smiled to himself at the naiveté of such thinking. But then, she had a way of presenting the impossible as practical.

Of course, she had made her dream into a reality. The brief visit to the Golden Owl Books and Brews proved as much. He'd noticed the handmade greeting cards and scented soaps, necklaces and earrings, and even the stage with its microphone waiting to showcase local talent. He'd spent a lot of time with her at the store. Yet, the store also kept them apart. He pressed his lips together to quell the rising irritation. What's done was done.

"Hasn't changed a bit." He parked the car in front of the gray stone building. Easing out of the car, he gazed up at the imposing façade.

How many times had he stood just so and stared at the storefront? A steady stream of reminiscences marched through his mind. Glimpses of himself as a boy of eight, ten, twelve, and most of all in his teen years. Sitting on a tall stool at the counter, licking the slowly melting ice cream from the side of the cone. Sucking on a milkshake, with the delicious gurgling sound as he dredged up the last glorious bits from the bottom of the glass. Slipping a quarter into the juke box and choosing a song to liven up the place. The awkward classmate behind the counter waiting on customers, his pimply face and shy smile making Leo feel as awkward as the boy had appeared. What was his name?

Concentrating hard, he recalled the kid wasn't a jock but excelled at Debate Team and Mathalogics Team. Thane. That's it. Where was he now? All grown up and moved away, no doubt. Moved on. Just like Leo had.

"Nothing ever seems to change around here." Roxie joined him on the sidewalk. "Look at that." She pointed to an immense oak tree shading the sidewalk.

Legend claimed the tree had been planted by the founder of the town more than two hundred years ago to honor his beloved wife. The tears of love and grief he'd cried while planting the tree, according to the storytellers, infused it with the power to defeat all threats to its existence. As a result, the townspeople believed that if a truly loving couple carved their initials into the tree, their love would endure forever. Silly as it might seem, even Leo had once believed in the myth.

"I can't believe it's still standing." He hurried to inspect the side of the trunk closest to the store. "Our initials are still there, too."

He'd been seventeen when he'd carved LK+RG into the rough bark. Head over heels in love with the girl then and now standing beside him, leaning close to look over his shoulder. He could feel her—not only the warmth of her supple body, but her breath, her heartbeat—as she lingered for several seconds. He stared at the hole a smidge above eye level, where bluebirds nested year after year, rather than indulge in drinking in her beauty. When she straightened away from him, he automatically leaned toward her, keeping her close, before abruptly pulling back. He had to control his impulses. He wasn't staying no matter how fondly he recalled their time together. Their time had passed. He forced himself to walk toward the lone step up and into the store even though she hadn't moved. He pulled open the door, waiting.

She met his gaze, started toward him, and then glanced back at the tree. "I wonder…"

She spun and hurried to the oak, shoving her hand into the nesting hole and patting around inside. A likely place to hide a small package. But also a place associated with family, home, new beginnings, love. All symbols of their friendship. Curious, he let the door swing shut and marched back to where she stood. Pulling her hand out, she grimaced.

"Let me try." Ignoring the warning voice about what poisonous critters might lurk inside the cavity, he reached in and felt around. Twigs and feathers and fluff but no package. He pulled his hand out and brushed it on his jeans. "Nothing. It must be inside the drug store somewhere."

"I have this feeling…" She continued staring at the tree, a puzzled frown marring her lovely features. She snapped her fingers and aimed a brilliant smile his way. "Together."

She grabbed his hand and plunged their joined hands into the nesting place. The contact sent a thrill straight to the center of his being as she maneuvered their hands around inside the tree. He didn't much care if they didn't find anything, as long as the intriguing sensation continued. Distracted by her nearness, her scent combined with her allure, he found himself smiling.

Across the street, he spotted a man in dark blue overalls with a forest green shirt and brown boots loitering on the corner, watching them. The weathered face was the color of dried tobacco leaves, suggesting he'd spent a lot of time outdoors. His long black hair was pulled back into a ponytail draped over one shoulder. He didn't move yet his pants and tee shirt seemed to shift gently around him. Even from that distance, the man's crystal blue eyes bored into Leo with a knowing gleam. Leo's smile faded when the man folded his arms over his chest and lifted his chin to look down his long pointed nose at him. At that moment, a noisy pickup hauling a trailer of bawling beef cattle rattled past. When it turned the corner and Leo looked across the street again, the man was gone. He scanned left and right but saw no one like the strange man, only the normal townsfolk hurrying about their business.

"Aha!" Roxie released his hand and pulled hers out of the tree. On her palm lay a small round silver box. "Found it."

Startled and uneasy, Leo brought his attention back to Roxie. She held it so calmly and yet he suspected the object could end up being more than it appeared. Shoving his hands in his front pockets, he stared at the small container. "Enchanted?"

"Absolutely. She apparently made it so only we could find it. Nobody else would have discovered it if they'd tried." She carefully lifted the lid off the box and handed it to Leo. A gold charm with the word "Friends" lay on top of a folded gold paper. "We were right. The riddle was about us being friends." She held out her left wrist with the charm bracelet glinting in the early afternoon sunlight. "Put it on, won't you?"

"How? I don't have the right tools."

"I doubt you'll need them." She smiled knowingly as she motioned to him to pick up the charm. "Bring it close to the chain."

He did as requested, being careful to avoid as much as possible letting his fingers rest on her velvety skin. As the charm neared the bracelet, it melded to the loops of its own accord. Leo blinked at the attached charm, then drew in a sharp breath. "Did you see that?"

"Yeah, it glowed. Like it did at Amber's." She fingered the word charm and then let it dangle beside the book charm. "I thought I'd imagined it back at the café, a trick of the lighting or something."

"That's some spell your mother cast." He shouldn't be surprised knowing how powerful Peggy Golden had been.

In fact, the most powerful witch in the Order. "What's the note say?"

Roxie retrieved the paper and handed the box to Leo. He snapped the lid closed and inspected the tiny box while she unfolded the paper.

"Interesting. I don't have a clue what this means. Listen."

Two facing forward while moving back
Building a bridge to tomorrow
As strong and unbreakable
As faith and hope combined.
What am I?

"Your mom was not a poet. She should have asked you to help her write these things."

Roxie laughed and folded the note. Taking the box back, she put both into her bag and zipped it closed. "But she sure can write riddles. Let's go."

"Where?" He aimed a quizzical frown at her. "Aren't you going to discuss the clue?"

She shook her head and winked at him. "Nope. I have a much better idea."

Chapter Four

"**W**hat's your idea?"

"Simple." Roxie settled the red bag more comfortably on one hip. "Take me to get my car and you go on back to Twin Oaks. I want to curl up with a book and a glass of wine and think about all that's been happening. Alone."

"I thought you said we had to do this quest together. Now you want to separate?" He frowned at her, tilting his head to one side as he studied her.

"As long as we're in the same town, we should be fine." She shrugged away his concern. "Aren't you tired after being out in the sun most of the day? I know I am." She wanted a good long soak in the tub, then a bite to eat. Without any company.

She needed time to think, mull, meditate. Too many images, impressions, and experiences in one day to process. Especially with the distraction from Leo's continued presence. How was she supposed to concentrate with his seesawing emotions so close by? Her empathic abilities could be useful but could also overwhelm her when someone experienced an intense emotion for an extended period. With Leo, she sensed him being standoffish one moment, attentive and eager the next. Glimmers of affection offset by flashes of resentment. No, she needed peace and quiet, and a fruity cabernet.

"Let me buy you dinner." He glanced away and back, as if unsure of her reaction to his offer. "If you're hungry, I mean."

Starving, but she'd much rather have some quiet time to herself. She started to squash any ideas he had of spending the evening with her when her cell phone played its tune and she stared at the screen. "Hold that thought. It's Meredith. Hey, what's up?"

"Are you with Leo?" Meredith's voice floated on the still afternoon air. "Tell me you're with him, please?"

"Yes, he's right here."

"I need you to bring him back to Twin Oaks as soon as possible. I've got to make some other arrangements for him for the night. Can you make that happen?"

Roxie sighed as she recognized the efficient, no nonsense tone. Her tantalizing bath plans flowed swiftly down the drain. "We're on our way. See you soon."

Leo unlocked the car as Roxie led the way to it. "Where are we going?"

"Twin Oaks. Something's up." Roxie settled into the passenger seat as Leo hurried to get in and start the engine. "I'm afraid our plans are about to change whether we want them to or not."

Twenty minutes later Leo pulled into the long drive leading up to the two-story Greek revival manor. The plantation had become a second home for her and her sisters. Roxie skimmed the pair of ancient oak trees, the inspiration for the name Twin Oaks, flanking the red brick house with its four large columns spaced across the front porch. A flock of ducks occupied the banks of the large lake, its surface reflecting the blue sky above. Leo parked the car at the end of the sidewalk and they sped up the front steps to the wide porch. The front door opened as they approached to reveal Meredith carrying a battered Braves duffle bag in one hand.

"What's going on?" Roxie gave Meredith's shoulders a light squeeze of an embrace and then peered at her.

"Here's your overnight bag, Leo." She shoved the duffle at him until he took it and then shrugged. "You'll need to stay with Roxie tonight because the electricity is out here. Since you're our only guest at the moment, we're closing down operations until the electrician can come out tomorrow morning."

Leo stared at Meredith for a long moment, slowly blinking as he processed the sudden need for his abrupt departure from the historic property. Straightened his spine as if preparing for battle. "You intend for me to stay with Roxie?"

Roxie stiffened in response to his resistance to the idea. She hadn't wanted to invite him to stay with her for a reason. Yet his defensive reaction put her on edge. She wanted to refuse but her cousin looked adamant. Still, she had to try to dissuade Meredith from insisting on the already settled course of action for both Leo's and her own sake. "Is that really necessary? Surely he could sleep here despite the power outage."

"Exactly." Leo nodded, glancing between Roxie and Meredith. "I can rough it."

Meredith propped a hand on one hip and gave them a sly grin. "Sorry, but no deal. Max and I discussed it and we're in agreement. With Paulette and Zak off to Knoxville for the night, we'll have the place to ourselves for one precious night for once in a blue moon."

Roxie regarded the light of anticipation in Meredith's gaze. "I'm thinking candles will be involved?" Roxie chuckled at her cousin as a growing dread spread through her core. The smile on Meredith's face spoke volumes about how she awaited the romantic evening ahead. Roxie quelled any of her own resistance. She'd give her cousin a night with her husband even if it meant a night alone with her ex. She'd survive. "Okay, you win. Come on, Leo, let's leave the love birds to it."

"You're caving, Roxie? Figures. See you tomorrow, Meredith." Leo's farewell sounded petulant as he trudged back down the brick steps, tossing his bag in the back seat before sliding into the driver seat. "Ready?"

Roxie eased into the car and pulled the door closed. Knowing they would spend the night together in her house turned the luxurious vehicle into an emotionally charged too-small space. Despite their past, or maybe because of it, an awkward silence fell between them as he headed for downtown Roseville.

Roxie thought hard and fast about the proper arrangements once they arrived. He'd never stayed at the Golden home. Visited many times for a friendly cookout or festive holiday meal. But he'd had no reason to sleep over when they'd dated. Her mother wouldn't have permitted him to hang out late enough to force him to stay. She'd put him in her mom's old room which she'd converted into a guest bedroom with its own bathroom. He'd be too close to her room, but she couldn't do anything about the proximity within the confines of her home.

"Still hungry?" Leo glanced at her and then back at the road. "We could stop at the Hideaway on our way through town."

"It's not necessary. I can throw something together when we get home." She shivered at the idea of sharing a house together. Even temporarily. She cast a quick glance his way but he didn't look at her, instead keeping his eyes on the road.

"I'll buy. Save you the trouble so late in the evening." He raised a brow at her and smiled. "I know I could eat."

"You don't have to buy. It's okay." Did she want to sit across from him over a casual meal at the popular restaurant? In front of everyone. They'd surely recall how the pair had been so close years before and then assume Leo and Roxie were a couple again. Wrong. She could hear the rumor mill wheels churning with the mere idea of being seen together for dinner out.

"Come on, Roxie. We're here and we're hungry." He parked in front of the Hideaway and shut off the engine. "Be reasonable for a change."

She glared at him. Considered staying put rather than entering the restaurant as if they had reunited. Which would make her look childish and churlish. Her stomach growled softly, evidence of the growing hunger she had tried to deny. Defeated, she pushed open her door with a low grunt of annoyance. "Fine. If you insist."

He came around to close the door for her as she stepped onto the sidewalk. "I do."

Inside the brightly lit restaurant, several tables of customers paused to glance at them as the waitress led them to their seats. The other customers smiled briefly and then resumed their conversations. What she'd feared had not happened. Yet. She followed Leo to a blond wood table in the back of the restaurant. On the wall above the bar hung a jackalope, the mythical animal created by adorning a jack rabbit with antelope horns. The bartender looked young and strong as he reached for a martini glass from the rack hung above the bar. A couple of men sat on the tall chairs, leaning on the bar and sipping their beers while watching a Braves game on the TV mounted on the wall. A typical Saturday night in a small town. Her small town.

She turned back when she realized Leo wasn't beside her. He lingered at the end of the bar, his rapt attention on the baseball game. "Leo?"

He blinked and swiveled his gaze her direction. With a tip of his head toward the game, he strode toward her. "They're losing. If I'd been there…"

"You will be soon." Did he have to remind her at every opportunity of his longing to be far from his hometown? "Come on."

Seated at the table, she perused the flimsy menu and then laid it aside. Leo chewed briefly on his lower lip as he nodded once and set his menu on top of hers. Then he smiled at her, somewhat sheepishly, as the waitress stopped to take their orders. She was back in a flash with their sweet teas and then vanished into the kitchen.

Roxie hadn't seriously looked at him since he'd sprung back into her life. With him sitting across from her, she could see the small differences the years had made. He'd clipped his black hair rather short, much shorter than before. Barely brushing his ears but it made him seem older, more mature. His amber eyes had tiny lines radiating from the corners but they still were warm and sigh worthy. His strong jaw displayed a touch of stubble. Would it be rough under her fingertips? She dropped her hands to her lap as insurance against unwanted touching.

More than physical changes sat upon his shoulders, though. Which were broad and muscled but also seemed to carry a sense of purpose. The angle of his head as he watched her indicated patience and self-assurance. His slightly curled lips invited her kiss. Her lips parted in response to the thought and she snapped them closed again. Nope. No kissing. No touching. No nothing. He'd made it abundantly clear through words, actions, and feelings they would not go back to their past relationship.

"Like what you see?" He winked at her with a slow smile spreading onto his mouth.

The kind of smile he'd worn when about to seduce her. About to take her in his arms and kiss her until her eyes closed and the world vanished. Only the two of them existing for precious moments. The warmth of his lips on hers, his tongue delving into her mouth and igniting a slow-burning fire in her nether region. His arms wrapped around her, supporting her as she melted under his intense heat. The memory proved enough to light a spark but she crossed her legs to contain the sensation.

"Not too shabby, I'd say." She unwrapped her silverware, removing the white paper band and folding it over and over until it resembled a flat straw.

"The view from here is pretty fine." He lifted his glass to take a long swallow of iced tea. "If I haven't said already, I think you've done exactly what you set out to do with the store. Congratulations."

"The expansion?" Roxie grunted softly and glanced at the bartender where he shook a cocktail shaker with noisy enthusiasm. Bringing her gaze back to meet Leo's, she fiddled with the paper in her fingers. "Right before Mom died we all agreed to try it."

"Has it been a hit?"

"Very much so. I can't imagine not including the local artists." She'd arranged for Tara to be in charge of the evening's performances. As hostess, Tara would provide the refreshments to the crowd that had surely gathered to root on the handful of people brave enough to step up to the microphone and read a poem or play a song. The three sisters took turns playing hostess for the events. "I'm sure tonight's open mic went as well as the rest. The local people love to encourage each other."

"Are you still happy living in Roseville?" He rested one elbow on the table, his fingers loosely holding the sweating glass. "Still never going to leave?"

"I don't want to leave but that's not the only reason I stay." His real question centered on why she wouldn't agree to follow him as he pursued his dream of hitting the major leagues. She'd wished him well, but simply couldn't go with him. Which broke her heart. "I love my town almost as much as my family. We belong here."

He nodded slowly, then sat back as the waitress arrived with their dinner. Country fried steak and mashed potatoes with a side salad for him, and fish and chips and slaw for her. Roxie doctored her fish with tartar sauce as she waited for his reaction. He had not taken her reasons well last time so she doubted he'd accept them now.

He forked some potatoes and held it aloft as he studied her for a moment. Swallowing the bite, he shook his head. "My father said something similar but I disagree. This town needs to wake up, grow up. There's so much more to do in Atlanta. So much more opportunity for improvement and success. I can't wait to go back where I belong."

A wave of strong emotion washed over her as he stared at her. Denial and fear battled with the hope in his soul. He wanted her to believe him even if he didn't believe what he'd said. Perhaps his true emotions were what he denied even to himself. But what did he fear and for what did he hope?

"If you're happy there, then I'm happy for you." She placed a bite of hot white fish in her mouth and savored the contrast of flavors provided by the delicately fried coating and the sweet mayonnaise sauce. She kept herself open to his churning intensity, sifting and sorting through his emotions as she chewed and swallowed. "But I think you do belong here."

"It's not important." He contemplated her for a minute. "I should let it go, but it still hurts that you wouldn't come with me. We could have made it work."

She sighed as she considered his statement. He still didn't understand. Even though he came from a magical family, he couldn't or wouldn't comprehend the necessity for the Golden and the King families to be loyal to the

Order. Peggy Golden and Homer King had ruled like queen and king over the Order of Witchery Lore, ensuring the safety and completeness of the collection of literature associated with magic and spellcraft. The history of their people and the labor of love to manage and preserve the thousands upon thousands of books, recordings, movies, and so much more. Even if she wasn't actively involved, she still supported the mission and the purpose of OWL by tending to the offerings of the bookstore and guiding customers to find the books and information they needed, longed for. Employed her gifts to help others in both obvious and subtle ways.

She laid her fork down on her plate. "We can't change the past."

"No, but we do have some say over our future." He dropped his fork onto the plate with a tinny clang. "We could have tried."

They had tried and yet failed. He'd chosen himself and his goals over them as a couple. He'd made his choice to risk everything OWL stood for by using his magic to benefit himself. When he'd gone so far as to tell her about his indiscretion with such pride she knew he needed to be reined in. His ego had overstepped his moral sense. She'd confided in her mother about his bragging of using his mind control power to force the coach to select him to the varsity team, and subsequently ensuring his place on the all-county and all-state teams. With the intent of being chosen for the major leagues straight out of high school. An unlikely scenario but one he planned to arrange. He'd brought his ultimate downfall on himself.

"I've lost my appetite." She dabbed her lips with the paper napkin and then pushed away from the table. "Let's go get my car and go to the house."

She couldn't even call it home while he stayed there. His negative energy would suck the comfort from the very walls.

But she wouldn't argue with him any longer. No point in rehashing past decisions and their ramifications. Not in public nor in private.

"Sit down and finish your dinner." Leo gestured to the barely touched fish. "We're not done."

His tone sounded much like a parent scolding a child. One thing she most definitely was not was a child. She stared at him for three rapid beats of her heart. He lifted a brow, expecting compliance with his unreasonable demand. The absolute last straw.

She pushed her chair in with a crash against the table and turned to leave without waiting for him. She'd walk the few blocks to the café and her car. Leave him to wallow in his self-indulgence. A scrabble behind her told her he'd risen quickly and followed. Felt him closing the space between them. She didn't look back as she pushed out the front door and onto the street.

"Roxie, wait." Leo appeared at her side, breathless and frowning. "I'm sorry. I didn't mean to upset you."

"I think you did." She lifted her chin and lengthened her stride, but he grabbed her arm to bring her to a halt. She jerked her arm but he held fast. "Let go."

"Don't walk away. I'm sorry." He released her arm and she stepped back. "I'll take you to your car and then follow you home. Okay?"

"You're a selfish man. You do what pleases you and then expect people to do what you want just because you want it." Roxie dragged in a calming breath, blowing out the irritation along with it. If they were to exist peacefully together in the house for the night, she had to find some way to calm her anger. Staying riled up would only make her off-center and sick at heart. But he needed to understand why she'd walked away in the first place. She raked a look over his concerned features. "As long as you *never* try to tell me what to do again, you may stay in my house. Clear?"

He grimaced and shrugged. "I'll do my best."

"You best succeed." She huffed and then pivoted on her heel. She marched back to his car, ready to put the matter behind her. If only he'd let sleeping dogs lie. They'd get along fine. Only, she had a strong feeling she hadn't heard the last of his anger over events of the past.

The Victorian style house with its wraparound porch and gingerbread woodworking renewed his guilt and shame. Returning to the place where he'd been stripped of all his powers, brought all the old grievances to the forefront of his memory. His prodigious memory never forgot any detail of his encounters, of his conversations. Of anything. His mind once had enormous power which his father had started to grow concerned about. Leo could not only read others' minds but manipulate them to his bidding. And his burgeoning ability to move objects went undeveloped as a result of his mistake. Roxie's reminder of his selfish behavior, not only then but still, stirred up the nearly constant emotional pain he recalled from his reprimand.

Leo forced himself to remain calm, but each unwilling step along the flagstone sidewalk toward the pale yellow walls with brown trim proved a Herculean effort. Objectively, the house stood as a fine example of pleasing architecture. On a personal level, however, he dreaded the moment when Roxie pulled open the back door and they entered the kitchen. Flipping a light switch, she set her purse on a small shelf by the door.

"Welcome to my home." Roxie crossed the small kitchen to the sink where she shoved several coffee cups into the dishwasher. Flashing him a rueful smirk, she closed the door and turned to lean against the counter. "Sorry. I wasn't expecting company."

He waved off her apology as he looked around the cheerful kitchen. The small island with cupboards beneath held a set of canisters for flour and sugar. A bookcase at the rear of the kitchen displayed an eclectic mix of titles, everything from poetry to essays, mysteries, and classics. A table covered with a flowered cloth and four cushioned chairs took center stage.

The closed door on the opposite wall led to the scene of his castigation. The living room with its floral carpet, framed photographs on the walls and tables, and a sofa and wing-backed chairs. He closed his eyes against the image of him standing in front of the roaring fireplace while Peggy Golden wove a convoluted spell and then touched him with her gnarled wand on both of his shoulders. A searing pain had flashed through him as she bound his powers. He'd cried out at the injustice as well as the agony then collapsed to the floor, unconscious. When he came to, he'd felt incomplete, weak, and immature. Years passed before he felt close to whole again. More time passed while he built up his strength and speed to the demands necessary for his chosen profession. Then he'd come back to the town, the very house, and all the old insecurities and weaknesses threatened to undo everything. His stomach rolled over and lay like a rock inside.

"You okay?" Roxie straightened to ease toward him. "You look kinda pale."

"Could I have a drink?" He mentally chased away the rush of memories. "Something strong."

"Sure. We can go out to the conversation corner and stare at the stars." She marched out of the room and came back a few minutes later with two tumblers of amber fluid. "Jack Daniels on the rocks."

"Perfect." He gripped the glass and gulped once, letting the warmth flow down his throat. "That's good."

"My fave." She nodded and eased past him to flip on the outside light. "Come on."

Soon they were seated around the crackling fire pit on a circular brick patio in the far corner of the privacy fenced backyard. Flowering roses and other vines climbed the slatted boards, perfuming the evening air. Above, the night sky twinkled with stars and a sliver of a moon. A perfect night and yet he felt decidedly imperfect, found wanting on every level. He laid his head back and glowered at the faraway points of light.

"Do you remember the last time I was here?" The words blurted from his mouth before he could stop them. He kept his gaze on the sky, not wanting to see her reaction. Not daring to see sympathy or, even worse, pity in her beautiful eyes.

"Yes." She shifted in her seat but didn't say anything more.

He peered at her through half-closed eyelids, saw her looking away from him and toward the garden shed off to one side with a workbench under an overhanging roof. "What happened after…?"

She shook her head and then looked at him, a fierce light in her eyes. "I don't want to discuss it. The past can't be changed."

"What *do* you want to talk about?"

"Must we talk? Just enjoy the evening." She sipped her drink and let her gaze drift away to survey the flower beds and patches of Pampas grass at intervals around the manicured yard.

Silence settled between them. If she refused to talk, then he'd clear his thoughts entirely. Stare up at the distant points of light and not think. Just be. Float amidst the sensation of the soft cushion beneath his tense body. Listen to the crackling fire. Smell the aroma of burning wood over the sharp tang of the whiskey in his glass. But not think.

No concerns about the past, the future, and definitely not about the present. Sitting so close to her and yet light-years apart in so many ways. She was right they couldn't change the past, but they could try to understand it. Discuss why she'd ratted on him instead of being proud of his ability to achieve one simple goal. Everyone knew it wasn't what you know but who that makes the difference in life. He wanted to make sure the talent scouts knew his name and would give him the opportunities he craved in order to prove himself. He hadn't needed special powers to be an exceptional pitcher. He only used a nudge to open the door for him.

A car door slammed and moments later Beth hurried into sight carrying several bulging tote bags over one arm. She waved at them but continued into the house.

Uneasy with the prolonged lull in conversation, Leo chose to broach a new topic. "When did Beth meet Mitch?" He sipped the whiskey, enjoying the taste and the slow burn in his throat. "They seem quite a good pair."

"A few months ago when Mitch came into town on an airplane repo assignment." Roxie rested her glass on her knee. "Beth fell in love with his job before she fell in love with him."

"What's that supposed to mean?"

Chuckling, Roxie swished the amber fluid in her glass. "She went on a fitness and self-defense kick and then got kidnapped."

"She what?" Leo sat up straight and leaned forward, cradling his glass between his hands. "That's crazy."

"Absolutely. Mitch went after her and brought her home safe and sound. It was quite an interesting summer."

"That's why she fell in love with him? Because he rescued her?"

"Oh, he didn't rescue her. She rescued herself and a young boy. He just flew her home in a fighter jet." Roxie smirked at Leo's shocked expression. "Like I said, quite an adventure for her. But she's come to realize life here in town can be more fulfilling than putting herself and others at risk."

He caught a chiding tone in her statement. Directed at Beth or him? Had Beth been dissatisfied with life in the sleepy little town like him? After all, he made no bones about the fact he didn't want to live in Roseville any more than he wanted to swim in peanut butter. A town replete with nosy neighbors and small town ideas. Both of which had caused him pain and shame and encouraged his hasty departure from said town. A tiny voice pestered him by adding the sleepy town included Roxie, a very good reason for wanting to move back. He hushed the inner voice.

"What boy? How did he get home?"

"The boy is the son of Beth's martial arts instructor. Jo had flown with Mitch to go after Beth and Arthur. The FBI brought them home."

"Beth really got serious about self-defense, doing Brazilian Jiu-Jitsu, I mean." Leo fumbled for the words to convey his surprise and awe. "That's a tough sport for a woman."

"You don't want to mess with her." Roxie laughed out loud. "She's lethal, I'm told. Even Mitch treads carefully."

Leo laughed with her, his gaze dropping to her left hand and then away. No ring. He hadn't until that moment even wondered if she were seeing someone. But even without a ring she could be serious about someone. How many others had she dated since him?

The unwanted image of her with another man, a faceless, nameless man, loomed in his mind. Holding hands as they walked down the street. Unafraid to demonstrate their love for each other for all the townsfolk to witness. Stopping at the courthouse square to sit in the shade of the gazebo. Kissing and whispering together. Their heads touching as he traced her cheek and jaw with a finger before planting a kiss on her luscious lips.

Or maybe they'd gone hiking together like he and Roxie used to enjoy. Out among nature. The stately swaying trees. A chuckling creek with tadpoles darting among the gently flowing water. Peering into the upper branches for the source of a particularly beautiful bird song. Spotting the delicate petals of wild daisies in the mottled shadowy forest floor. Taking her hand to help her up a steep part of the rock-strewn path. Receiving her kiss of thanks for the help.

Or maybe the guy she found interesting took her in his beefy pickup truck up to the overlook for some old-fashioned necking. More aware of each other than the twinkling lights of the valley below. Maybe even in the very parking space he'd always considered theirs.

Was she actually seeing someone now? The question burned in his brain but he had no right to ask. Yet it sizzled in his mind, tempting him to inquire as to her status. But he couldn't. Shouldn't. Think. Anything else but that.

"The riddle. What do you think it might mean?" Better. He blinked at her as he waited for her reply.

She set her glass on the arm of the chair and studied him for several seconds. "I've been pondering it, but haven't sorted it out."

"What was the first line again?" He knew the line, but wanted to hear her say it. Needed to hear her lilting, soothing voice give them a natural starting point for the discussion.

"I think it was 'two facing forward while moving back.' Odd, isn't it?"

"Facing forward but moving backward?" He frowned, screwing his mouth to one side as he pondered the riddle. Having perfect memory didn't mean he understood everything perfectly. "Very odd idea."

"Maybe not backward in direction, but back to another state." She leaned forward to rest her elbows on her knees. "Like from friends to enemies. Or happy to sad."

"Possible." He rubbed his forehead to ease the building tension. The day had been long and convoluted both mentally and emotionally. Pressing on his sinuses only made the throbbing worse, pulsing over his eyes in pounding waves. "I can't think about this anymore. I'm getting a headache."

"I'm not surprised. It's been quite a day." She straightened and stood, motioning with her free hand for him to follow. "I'll show you where you're sleeping."

For a fleeting second his addled brain wondered if she meant with her. More startlingly vibrant scenes arose in his mind. He quickly brushed them away, or tried to. The echo of the impressions lingered. Get a grip, man.

He rose to his feet and trailed after her up the stepping stone sidewalk and into the house. A sense of well-being settled in the pit of his stomach, a new and oddly comforting sensation. His head pounded so much he squinted against the pain which seemed to flow down into his gut for a moment. He dragged in a shaky breath and blew it out as he followed her. The deeper pain eased with each step until dissipating entirely. Leaving only the pulsing in his brain. Hopefully, sleep would vanquish the headache once and for all. He'd never had a tour of the house so had no idea where she was leading him. But her fine figure enticed him to follow, which he did quite happily.

After securing the door and turning off the outside light, she set their glasses in the sink and led him through the other door. He grabbed his duffel from the chair by the table and followed her into the hall. He ignored the scene of his shame as they passed the open living room door, and upstairs to a large bedroom with a private bathroom. The décor provided a cool pale yellow and white color scheme. A patchwork quilt on the bed and gold drapes at the window gave the only dashes of color. Thankfully, no frills and flowers in the decorations.

Nothing to make him think of her. He might even get some much needed rest.

"I hope you sleep well." She gazed at him silently for a moment. "If you need anything, I'm right next door." She pointed to the next room down the hall and then started to saunter in the same direction. "Night."

Damn. Now he'd likely not sleep a wink, not with her in bed on the other side of one measly wall. Within earshot. A few strides away. Not nearly far enough for his peace of mind. Then a wicked thought floated into his befuddled brain. What might she wear? A nightgown? Tee and shorts? A teddy? Or… The next thought tantalized and tormented in equal measure. Nothing? Though he'd never actually seen her naked, he had a vivid imagination. Perhaps too vivid. He swallowed hard as she paused at her open door, the light from inside adding a soft glow to her face and hair as she smiled gently at him.

"You okay?"

He nodded slowly, envisioning too many interesting possibilities involving his hostess. "I'm fine. Good-night."

Liar.

Chapter Five

The little settling-in sounds from her unexpected guest barred Roxie from relaxing. Footsteps thudded softly, moving around and pausing, then starting again. Leo preparing for bed. Water running in the bathroom. Brushing his teeth? Washing his face? Droplets of water clinging to the stubble on his jaw? She swallowed hard at the image. Stop. She had to stop her wayward imaginings. The water cut off and then more footsteps. The zipper on his duffel. The rustle of the hand-pieced quilt her grandmother had made for her mother's wedding gift so many years ago. Silence for a short span before the click of the bedside lamp being turned off.

Then the flow of his emotions started seeping into her mind and heart. She'd damped down the intensity while they sat outside earlier but after they parted at his bedroom door she'd decided to touch base again. Check in on how he was dealing with being in her home. She expected his disquiet, his uneasiness with being in the house. She hadn't expected his searing desire, his need for her, rolling and churning into her room, reaching out to her, enveloping her heart and soul. The contradiction between his words and his feelings tussled inside him and by extension inside her.

She couldn't stand it. Thinking of him next door, in bed, so close and yet so unreachable. Both emotionally and physically. She changed from her day clothes into a dark blue silky nightgown and a flowered robe. Sliding her feet into slippers, she padded down the hall to the bathroom she shared with Beth—for only another month, then she'd have the house to herself—to wash up before trying to sleep. So many changes happening all at once made her head swim. She had little hope of falling asleep with so much swirling in her thoughts.

Beth had closed her door, an uncharacteristic act as she preferred the gentle flow of air while she slept. She likened it to the house blowing her kisses. A quirky thought. With Leo in the house, she probably thought it more proper to keep the door closed. Definitely more private.

Roxie continued down the hall and into the bathroom, aware of the difference in the feel of her home. Having Leo within its walls seemed to make her house vulnerable. Waiting. Watching. Holding its breath. She shook off the odd sensation and quickly brushed her teeth and washed her face. Overlaid the image of Leo doing the same only minutes earlier, which didn't calm her thoughts one tiny bit. Her imagination was running away with her.

Back in her bedroom, she pushed the door closed with a snick of sound. Stood for a moment, listening for any movement next door. Leo's robust snoring suddenly confirmed he'd fallen asleep. Chuckling softly while hoping he wouldn't continue snoring all night, she crossed her bedroom to the writing desk under the window. The Book of Secrets laid open to the last spell she'd worked on. She closed the large, thick book and stored it safely on a lower shelf. Since she was wide awake, she may as well work on the riddle.

She opened her cross-body bag and pulled out the second box, retrieved the gold paper, and perused its contents for several minutes.

Two facing forward while moving back
Building a bridge to tomorrow
As strong and unbreakable
As faith and hope combined.

"What are you indeed." Roxie studied the lines carefully.

Her mother and her intentions remained a mystery as to why she'd cast such a powerful quest spell. Forcing the two of them back together to see it through. Had her mother considered the enchanted charms would have to survive for years before Roxie would even know they existed? She pondered again her mother's motivation. What did she know about her and Leo's destiny but never revealed to Roxie? Were they linked in some way? And why? Until she and Leo managed to finish collecting all the charms they would never know the reasons or the fate which awaited them. She glanced at the bracelet draped on her left wrist with its two charms. A book and the word Friends. What might the third one be?

Next door, Leo snorted and then must have rolled over because blessed silence ensued.

She smiled as she read the first line again, taking each word, each phrase separately. "Two. The two of us."

Her mother had insisted the two of them must work together. Facing something while going back and building a bridge for the future. But going back to what or to where? Possibilities eddied through her mind. Back to their friendship. Back to where that friendship had been tested? If they could go back to such a place, would it somehow help to build a bridge to their future friendship? But where or when did her mother mean?

Then the next line. What did the "strong and unbreakable" equal to "faith and hope" mean? Like a strong chain perhaps. Or a rope. With faith plus hope creating belief in something or…someone. Aha.

A place where they passed a test and then created a strong means of moving forward as friends. She reread the riddle with a particular day in mind and the pieces slipped neatly into place.

"I know what you are." She grinned at the paper in her fingers. Now she had the key. Her mother's clever use of Leo and Roxie's childhood memories would help them solve the riddles. Hopefully without delay. Then Leo would have his greatest wish and be able to escape the confines of the small town. And with any luck, not break her heart all over again when he left. "I can't wait to tell Leo."

She pivoted to head to the door but then heard his snoring restart. Excited by her discovery, she grabbed the doorknob and turned it. Pulled the door open and stepped into the hall. He snorted and snored. She paused, hesitating to stride to his door and knock. She sighed the excitement out of her chest. She couldn't wake him. They'd had a long day, even if parts were fun. Let him sleep. She'd tell him over breakfast.

Closing the door, she returned the paper to its box and put both into the crimson bag. Still smiling over her discovery of the hidden key to solving the clues, she laid her robe at the end of her bed and kicked off her slippers. She'd settle down even if the Sandman never visited. Leo's snoring reached a crescendo before lowering in volume. The sound reminded her of her jovial and loving father, may he rest in peace. Not an awful sound to her ears like it could be for others.

She closed her eyes, a small smile lingering on her lips as she drifted off to sleep still pondering the life-changing memory the riddle had invoked.

Wiping steam off the mirror, Leo leaned closer to peer at his lathered face. He scraped the razor slowly and smoothly down his right jaw, then rinsed the shaving cream down the sink. The routine steadied him, helped him find his emotional balance before venturing down to the kitchen and Roxie.

He hadn't slept well. He awoke with the sheets twisted about his legs after a series of disturbing dreams featuring enormous pythons chasing him through a valley of redwood trees. Above his terrified head, flapping wings of eagle-sized bats swarming and swirling in the sky. When he thought they'd caught him, a black horse appeared before him. He'd leapt onto its back and the horse took off, flying into the sky on wide, silky black wings. Carried him swiftly out of reach of both the snakes and the bats and landed him safely on the sidewalk outside of the Golden home. What on earth did it mean?

One last scrape of the blade. Wiping remnants of shaving cream from his face with a washcloth, he paused to stare at himself in the partially fogged mirror. Feeling grumpy and out of sorts didn't bode well for the day ahead. He spotted the worry reflected in his eyes, felt it trembling in his heart. He squared his shoulders and finished cleaning up his razor, ready to confront whatever came at him. Leo didn't back down from a challenge. He rose to face the music. The challenge he faced, staring back at him from the mirror, involved his mind as well as his heart. Completing the quest spell may prove difficult but more so for his heart than his mind. Coming home meant risking everything else in his life. For what?

His father had once told him that running off to play ball was a waste of his talents. But then he'd been instrumental in putting those talents out of the picture. Leo had to resort to his own natural abilities in order to make a life and a career. He stared at himself in the mirror, pride swelling inside. He'd done it. On his own abilities and merits. No more leaning on magic or supernatural abilities. Just like he thought his dad would approve of if he had lived to see Leo as an adult. But Leo hadn't returned to town until it was too late to make amends with his dad, show him how successful he'd become despite any disadvantage stemming from not having his powers. Too late to even say goodbye to his father. But not too late to handle matters at hand.

His father's estate must be closed which proved a challenge in itself. Leo hadn't realized the many tentacles of finances and responsibilities his father maintained. So far, he'd only scraped the surface of the tasks required to settle outstanding debts and consolidate his accounts. Which only meant Leo couldn't escape small town life entirely for some time. Bringing him back to Roxie's proximity again and again. Raising the specter of their past love over and over. Could he do so without hurting either of them? Somehow he would have to find a way.

He huffed and shook his head, a wry smile creeping onto his lips. He needed to focus on what he could control. His stomach rumbled obnoxiously, shaking him out of his funk. The next order of business was finding hot coffee and food.

Minutes later he trotted down the steps and into the kitchen. Roxie hummed as she bent over the open oven door, sliding a broiling pan out with sizzling bacon strips to perfume the air. Making him drool. Both the sight of Roxie's beautiful backside and the smell of bacon. He'd always been rather fond of her butt and it had only improved over time. As she straightened, he shifted his gaze away before she caught him staring. Saw the coffee pot full of hot, delicious brew.

"Good morning." Leo moved farther into the room, stopping at the other side of the island from where she stood with the hot pan in both hands. "Can I help?"

"Grab a mug from the rack and help yourself to coffee. Do you still take sugar?" She placed the pan on top of the stove and piled the two hot pads on the counter nearby.

"No, I gave it up years ago." He sidled to the wooden rack mounted on the wall beside the coffee pot and selected a dark green mug. "Cut back on sugar and feel better as a result."

"You're a stronger person than I am." She smiled as she snagged a plate from the cabinet and started piling the bacon on it. "I don't think I could or would want to give up sugar entirely."

"If you had to, you'd find a way." He sipped the coffee, relishing the hot flavorful brew. He raised his mug in salute to Roxie. "You still make wonderful coffee."

"Thanks. It's my own blend, mixing three special kinds into one smooth combination." She carried the plate to the island and set it in the center. "Do you want eggs or pancakes with your bacon?"

"Pancakes, please." Beth interrupted as she strode briskly into the kitchen and snared a mug and quickly poured coffee. Dressed for work in a polo and slacks, she clutched her mug. "I don't have much time."

"Why the hurry?" Roxie shrugged lightly at Leo before going to the pantry to pull out the pancake mix.

Beth leaned against the sink and sipped her coffee, the pretense of casualness revealing her agitation. "I'm meeting Mitch at the store and then we're going into Huntsville to check out tuxes."

"Sounds like fun." Roxie retrieved a mixing bowl from the cupboard, then the milk and egg carton from the fridge. She studied her silently and then peered closer at her sister. After a single silent moment, she arched a brow. "So why are you so upset?"

"Mitch doesn't want to wear a tux at all, but he has to." Beth gripped her mug until her knuckles gleamed pale against her skin. "I want him to."

"Doesn't he have a say?" Roxie cracked a couple of eggs into the bowl with swift movements.

Leo followed Roxie's actions with increasing awareness of her beauty. She had matured into a lovely woman. He'd always thought her pretty but now she was absolutely gorgeous. Her beauty went far deeper than her appearance. Her grace, caring, and love for family radiated from her like an aura. Even without being able to read minds, he could still sense her inner beauty as a soft warmth on his skin. His core fluttered for a second, making him frown at the unusual disturbance. Odd.

"A traditional wedding calls for traditional attire." Beth wrinkled her nose and made a moue with her mouth. "I know how formal wear can be confining and even uncomfortable. But it's appropriate for the occasion. It's just that he's not so eager to put on a formal suit."

"If he doesn't want to wear one, why make him?" Leo tilted his head as he considered her for a moment.

He'd resist being dressed up without a really good reason. Not that he minded in general putting on a tailored suit and shined shoes. But overall he preferred casual to tux and tails. A dapper pinstripe suit, crisp white shirt, and fancy leather shoes would make a fine look for him. If he ever married. He'd only thought about doing so with one person six years ago. He glanced at Roxie stirring the ingredients into a thick batter with a wooden spoon.

"Like I said, it's traditional." Beth pinned her annoyed stared on Leo. "And because I just know he'll look magnificent in one."

"Leo has a point, sis." Roxie turned to lift the griddle from on top of the fridge, placing it on the island and plugging it in. "It's not a requirement to wear a tux."

"But I'll be wearing a gown, so he needs to match in formality." Beth drained her cup and held it with both hands. "Right?"

"It's your wedding." Roxie paused to press her hands on the counter while the griddle warmed.

Beth spun around to refill her mug, a slight tremor obvious as she lifted the carafe to pour. Leo suspected she needed a moment to compose herself after Roxie's subtle but pointed dig. Glancing at Roxie, he met her serious gaze and held it for several seconds. She really loved her family and held them close. But he could also tell she felt obliged, even though it had to be difficult, to teach her younger sister life lessons before she learned them the hard way. Roxie's concern for her family ran deep. But maybe she could use some help.

"Roxie makes a good point, Beth." Leo cleared his throat and then continued. "Have you bought your gown yet?"

"No…" Beth clutched her coffee mug in a death grip.

"Then it's not too late to rethink the kind of dress you will wear." Leo smiled at her, trying to ease her discomfort and open an avenue of conversation. "I'm sure you could find a beautiful dress and Mitch could wear a decent suit. Then you'd both be happy."

"What about tradition?"

Leo shrugged and relaxed back in his chair. "Isn't it also tradition that the bride gets to plan the wedding the way she wants?"

Beth stared at him as she sipped her coffee, obviously delaying her response. Finally, she lowered the mug. "I suppose I could."

Roxie mouthed "thank you" to Leo, making warmth blossom in his chest. Then she smiled at Beth. "I'd be happy to go with you to find the perfect dress." She started spooning batter onto the griddle, small circles of sizzling fragrant pancakes. "If you want me to, of course."

Beth leaned against the sink, cradling her mug in her palms. "We can make a girls day of it. Take Tara along too."

"Oh, better yet. Paulette's a clothing designer. Maybe she'd have time to make you something." Roxie turned the pancakes and pressed them lightly with the spatula. "Would you grab some plates, please?"

"Great idea!" Beth carried a short stack of plates from the cupboard and placed them next to the griddle. "I'll give her a call later. Anyone want apple juice?"

Leo raised a hand and smiled at her. "Me."

Roxie nodded in agreement as Beth crossed to the fridge to peer inside and find the bottle. She poured three small glasses and carried them to the table.

"In the meantime, I think I have solved the second riddle." Roxie transferred several pancakes to a plate and handed it to Beth. She glanced up to meet Leo's raised brows and wide eyes. "Last night while you were snoring."

"You did? I was?" Leo gripped the edge of the counter. Another step closer to ending the torture, both the exquisite torture of Roxie's nearness and the mysterious clues leading them to the next hiding place. "What does it mean?"

Roxie huffed and shook her head. "It means you were really tired last night and I'm glad you are well rested because we'll have a busy day."

"What? No, the riddle. What does it mean?" The woman confused him with her roundabout logic. Or was she merely joking with him like in the old days? He hesitated for a split second, contemplating what it would mean if they fell back into old habits. Relied upon their belief in themselves as a couple once again. He shut down the line of thought knowing he couldn't permit such a turn of events. Wouldn't backtrack any farther than necessary. "Spit it out."

Beth added bacon to her plate and then moved to the table and sat down. "Start at the beginning and walk us through it."

"Let me finish here and I will." Roxie carefully doled out the remaining pancakes between the last two plates. Handed one to Leo with a wave at the plate of bacon. "Eat up."

Impatiently, Leo snagged a handful of strips and plopped them on his plate. Then strode to the table to add butter and syrup. Anything to move along the train of thought. "Please, the suspense is terrible."

Roxie chuckled as she joined them at the table and doctored her pancakes, took a sip of juice. "Okay, here goes. The first line about two facing forward while moving back refers to that scary fun day out hiking in the park. Our folks had driven us out and we wandered off on our own. Do you remember, Leo?"

How could he forget such a horrifying day? He laid his fork down as the memories flooded his mind and tremors twitched his hands. "You mean when I slipped down onto the ledge overlooking a steep rocky slope that ended in the rushing river? I'll never forget it."

A hot, windy day with high humidity. Storms brewing in the west but the Goldens and he and his dad had decided to venture out to the Cumberland Plateau to have a picnic lunch. Do some hiking. Play some catch. He and Roxie were thirteen and fast friends. The group of kids divided up, the younger ones staying with the parents. His dad had cautioned him to look out for Roxie as they headed down a well-marked trail. But it ended up her looking out for him.

Roxie rested a hand on his wrist. "After teasing me about hanging back, you fell down out of sight. Scared me half to death."

He closed his eyes as the humiliation and terror swamped his senses. He'd been urging her to lean over and look down into the ravine. Acting all big, tough guy as he playfully tugged on her hand. Until his sneakers rolled on a twig and down, down, down he tumbled. Screaming and grunting with each revolution until he stopped on a tiny ledge, grabbing hold of gnarly roots on the dirt wall. The churning waters of the river below warned of broken limbs or worse. The rock strewn slope beneath his toes wouldn't feel much better if he started rolling down the steep incline. He learned two things in that moment. Small spaces and heights frightened him so he shook in his shoes. Couldn't move for fear of continuing the tumbling down into the river. If he'd had his more mature powers, the outcome would have been different. But as a new teenager, those abilities hadn't yet formed. He'd been helpless and afraid. He opened his eyes to slowly shake his head at her, hoping to clear away the remaining tendrils of the terror from his groggy mind.

"You? I was terrified." He swallowed hard, unable to tear his gaze from hers. "You saved my life. What was it you used to pull me up?"

He'd cried out to Roxie to find help. Do something to extricate him from the precarious position. He prayed for rescue. Pleaded with the saints and gods and anyone else he could think of to save him from certain death. Mostly, he relied on Roxie to find a solution. Trusted her to come to his aid.

"My belt and some wild vines, aided by a quick flick of my wrist to strengthen the knots." She squeezed his hand, sending sparks up his veins. A slight smile graced her lips. "See, we were both 'facing forward' at the time, until I pulled you 'back' up to be with me. I think the 'rope' is the bridge in the riddle which created our unbreakable bond. One born of your faith and hope I could rescue you."

She did, too. Managed to lower the lifeline he'd grabbed hold of and helped him creep back up the cliff he'd fallen down. One trembling, frightened step at a time. Only his faith in her gave him the courage to climb the sheer, daunting cliff. When he flung himself back onto the flat forest floor again, he'd lain still while taking deep breaths, thankful to be safe and alive. Pushed himself to his feet, and hugged his friend, clung to his savior for several minutes.

"I trusted you." He laid his free hand on top of hers and squeezed. One thing he knew in his heart of hearts. "I still do."

She pressed her lips together for a moment then nodded, eyes glittering. "Exactly. Mom knew how shaken you were by the whole incident. You didn't stop thanking me for saving your life for a month. You talked about it all the time. Nonstop, as I recall. Especially how you turned to me with faith and hope combined to believe in me. And you know what that means?"

He groped for the right response to her question. Thought over all they'd meant to each other. First as buddies, kids having fun together on their bikes or skating at the roller rink. Whatever they did and whenever they did it, they always enjoyed each other's company.

Then as middle school came their friendship deepened and he'd started to notice an almost visceral bond between them. Like he knew how she felt, how she'd react, without having to probe her mind. In fact, now that he thought about it, seventh grade was when they'd both realized they were especially talented. His mental prowess and her emotional and linguistic talents came to the fore. Made them unique from others, but similar to each other. That realization had cemented their link to one another.

Until finally in high school, they'd realized simultaneously their friendship had morphed into something much stronger, more meaningful, which could endure a lifetime of roller coaster rides. The day she hauled him up to stand at her side proved to be more than simply saving his life for one day. She'd saved it for them, to enjoy together forever.

"I think I do." A growing certainty filled Leo's chest like fresh air in a closed up house. He laid his hand on top of hers, stacking them like pancakes. A flutter in his gut startled him but he ignored it. Met her expectant gaze with a smile. "Time to go to the park."

Chapter Six

The parking lot for the Castle Rock trailhead looked remarkably the same as the last time she walked across its expanse. Her senses stood at attention as she stepped out of Leo's car, and paused to let her gaze drift across the area. All was quiet. Not even a bird chirped in the trees. Still, her probe picked up distant thoughts and feelings of concentration. Probably the park rangers hard at work, or perhaps play, in the visitor center. She grinned at the mental image of a ranger playing a Yogi Bear video game featuring Boo-Boo wearing his purple bowtie and the many forest creatures.

A rustic visitor station with a sign announcing the name of the area stood next to a small building housing the austere restrooms. The gravel loop of driveway included a dozen parking spaces in the center. At the path leading to the trail, a map of the length and direction of the trail was encased in glass on a sturdy pole. Roxie considered where an enchanted charm might be concealed. Not very many hidey-holes visible from her vantage point. Where would her mother have hidden it?

Leo joined her beside his red Corvette, his gaze scanning the area before meeting hers. "Want to try your magic first?"

"I don't think Mom wanted me to resort to shortcuts." She shot him a wry smirk. "At least it didn't work the last time I tried."

"Point taken. Then where do you think we should start?"

Roxie shook her head slowly, pondering possibilities. "Maybe the sign?"

"As good a place as any to begin with. And of course there's only one way to know. Come on." He started toward the sign with long, quick strides.

She hurried after him, excitement building inside with each step across the crunching gravel. "I hope it's there."

"Move this quest along." He halted at the sign, investigating potential hiding spots by leaning this way and that, walking around the large wooden sign with CASTLE ROCK TRAIL HEAD emblazoned on it in red letters. "Try here."

His reminder of the urgency he labored under sent a chill through her. She'd rather hoped he'd warm to the prospect of spending time with her. Chastened by her childish wishes thwarted, she moved to his side to peer at a crevice where a knot had once been on the back of the sign. "Give me your hand."

He did as asked and they reached in with their fingers into the small opening. The rough interior proved empty after only a second of searching with her fingertips. Still, she held on for a precious few more seconds before releasing his hand.

"Nothing." She heaved a sigh, both at failing to find the box and at her own weakness, and pointed to the front of the visitor center. "Let's try there."

After poking into several likely spots, they faced each other on the front porch of the building. She could tell from his quick scan of the area and tense shoulders he was annoyed at their lack of progress. Without a doubt, he would leave. He'd made his intentions crystal clear on more than one occasion. When he did, he'd break her heart all over again. She had to decide whether she'd let him or protect herself by keeping her distance. An easy choice.

Leo crossed his arms over his chest. "It has to be here. There's no other connection I can think of between the clue and our relationship."

"Agreed." She glanced to the map case across the clearing. "We haven't looked at the map. That actually would make sense, since it leads to where you fell. Come on." She trotted down the couple of stone steps to the gravel drive.

"If it's not there, we'll probably have to search every damn tree for it." Leo caught up to her and matched her quick pace.

Anticipation coursed through Roxie as they stopped at the map case. Searched each side until she spotted the clear plastic box containing pamphlet-sized trail maps. The box hung from the bottom of the map case, leaving a gap between the box and the pole. She grabbed Leo's hand and reached into the gap with eager fingers. Poked to the left and then to the right and stretched to touch the back. Nothing.

"Dang it." Roxie shook her head, her ponytail ending up splayed over one shoulder. "Now what?"

She searched their surroundings with a quick skim of her gaze, until she noticed a figure standing on the porch of the visitor center. In the exact spot they'd recently stood. No other car but Leo's occupied the parking lot. She squinted at the shadowy being. Nothing odd about jeans and tee shirt, low-heeled boots, floppy hat, and wooden hiking staff in hand. She'd guess it was a man but why was he keeping to the darkness of the porch? Something mystical pervaded her mind the longer she stared at him. Then he pressed his right hand to the center of his chest and she saw the glint of gold. She summoned her telescopic ability and zoomed in more closely on his right hand as he lifted it to press to the center of his chest. He wore only a gold pinky ring, luminous despite the shadows of the deep porch. She squinted to bring the center stone into clear focus. An indigo owl. She'd seen the symbol before. Not associated with the park, she was certain. Where then? The shadowy figure pointed toward the path beside her with a soft gleam of a smile. The niggling concern in her mind bloomed into shock.

She turned to Leo, grabbing his upper arm. "Do you see him?"

"Who?" Leo glanced about, eyes wide and searching from side to side. "Where?"

Roxie clutched his arm as she pointed with her other hand. "On the porch."

But when she looked again, the man had vanished.

"Where'd he go?" She frantically looked around but no other people were in sight. No other vehicles, not even a work truck parked behind the center. "I saw him."

"Who?" Leo frowned at her. "Are you sure?"

She nodded and then sighed. "He pointed to the trail. And Leo…"

"Something else?"

"He was wearing a pinky ring. An indigo owl."

Leo blinked slowly at her as he firmed his lips for an instant. "Right hand?"

She bobbed her head. "Not the first member I think I've seen."

He stiffened and crossed his arms. "I may have spotted one when we found the Friends charm."

"So there's more than one watching?"

"Yes." Leo dropped his arms, clenching his fists at his thighs. "What does it mean?"

"I don't know, but I think…He wants us to go back to the ledge."

"No…"

"Yes." Roxie snared his hand and held on tight. "Let's go."

"Under protest."

"Duly noted. Come on."

She dragged him along with her down the narrow dirt path littered with rocks and roots. No wildlife made sound or rustlings as they tramped doggedly toward the site where the accident had cemented their lifelong friendship. Their trust in each other. Some twenty minutes passed with only grunts of effort to climb a hill or keep from sliding down the other side. Leo reached back to help her up the steeper slopes as he'd always done. Only she didn't thank him with a kiss even though somewhat tempted to do so, knowing his emotional distance wouldn't want her to renew their tradition. Finally, Roxie stopped at the edge of the slope plunging over the edge of the cliff. A barrier had been erected to prevent others from falling down the side of the mountain. What better place?

Roxie tugged Leo to the post-and-rail fence and paused to inspect the loose joints. The cross rails rested in the open holes of the anchored posts. Not as sturdy as some fences, but more in keeping with the rustic nature of the park. And providing plenty of options for hiding a charm.

"I think we've found the spot." Roxie assessed Leo's demeanor at having returned to the place where he'd discovered his two greatest fears. "One of these joints may be the hidey-hole."

"Get it over with." Leo's features were set in hard lines as he stood at her side.

Without further delay, she guided their joined hands into the various holes on the posts. Poking and prodding one after another. Until finally, she gasped when their joined fingers discovered another small jewel box to pull out into the light.

She stared at the round box resting on his open palm, the burnished silver surface gleaming in the late morning sunshine. He met her smiling grin with a tense smirk of his own. Then slowly lifted the hinged lid to reveal a gold charm of two hands clasped together in a handshake resting on a square of gold paper. He picked up the charm, closed the lid, and handed the box to Roxie.

She met his inquisitive stare with a shake of her head, then glanced around the small clearing at the bend in the trail. Searched for any hint of the shadowy figure from the porch. Relaxing, she dropped her gaze to study the silver box.

"I wonder what the next clue is?" She fingered the small container, anxious to figure out the next step in the quest.

"We'll read it in a minute. Let me put this on the bracelet so we don't lose it." He indicated her left wrist with a flick of his free hand. "Then we can worry about the next one."

"Good idea." She held out her wrist so he could touch the charm to the chain. The bracelet and charms glowed for a moment, brighter than before, then the charm secured itself to the bracelet. A sudden realization swept through her. Could it be?

She thought back over the last couple of days. The first time she'd seen the heart-shaped box with its bracelet and charm inside. A coolness to the pieces of jewelry had seemed natural. Then Leo added the word charm and the bracelet glowed and warmed a bit. The most recent charm, the handshake, had increased both the amount of warmth and the brightness of the glow. The evidence seemed to prove her theory.

She studied the gold links and charms dangling docilely against her skin. For how long? "Leo, I think the bracelet is collecting power with each charm."

"Is that a good thing?" He glowered at the bracelet as she smoothed her fingers over each charm in turn. "Or should we be worried?"

"Mom may have intended for it to grow stronger as we complete each step of the quest. But I'm not sure, which does worry me." She studied the charms for another few moments and then grabbed hold of the box with both hands. "Let's find out what's next instead of fretting about what we can't possibly know yet."

"If you'll promise to let me know if anything weird starts happening with the bracelet." He regarded her steadily, a protective vibe radiating from his entire being. "Promise?"

"You'll be the second one to know." She chuckled mirthlessly and then opened the box to grab the note inside. "Let's see…"

One pretends another's feelings
The other actually feels
The third pays the price
And one repents.
What am I?

"I have no clue what this one is hinting at." Roxie frowned at the riddle and then shifted her gaze to regard Leo. "Do you?"

Leo grew rigid beside her as he gaped into her startled eyes. Gradually, the light in his eyes dimmed as his brows lowered. "I didn't realize your mother knew about that."

A chill wiggled down Roxie's back at the guilt suddenly reflected in his entire expression and pulsing in his heart. "What's the matter?"

Wracking her brain for any hints, she could only watch him. What had her mother known about to put him on edge? Who else but the two of them could be involved in the moment of importance to understand the clue? The more upset Leo appeared, the more frantic Roxie felt to try to grasp what memory he prepared to reveal. One she obviously wouldn't like to recall. One she may have suppressed for her own well-being and peace of mind. But what?

"I know the answer." He jammed his hands into his front jeans pockets. "But I hate to remind you of the biggest mistake of my life."

So close to losing her forever. Through his own stupid actions. He had no one to blame but himself for risking everything on a whim. He'd learned a lesson he'd never forget as a result of his blundering.

"What are you talking about?" Roxie shifted her weight to one hip as she regarded him with a wary cast to her countenance. "What mistake?"

Leo shrugged, a defensive, buying-time move. He dreaded reminding her of what he'd done but he could tell from her stance and her frown he best start spilling his guts. He fisted his hands in his pockets.

"Do you remember when I told you about Hans Weber?" He chewed his lower lip and watched the recognition of the name settle in her expression. "The practical joke I played on him. That backfired."

The son of a fellow member of OWL, Hans was a pimply stick of a teen. Average in height, personality, and intelligence. Look up mediocre in the dictionary and you'd see his photo. The one thing he excelled in was long-distance running. He had the speed and stamina of a cheetah. He'd proven a worthy adversary for Leo's own burgeoning preternatural speed. The kid also had the tendencies of a bull dog. Once he latched onto an idea, he wouldn't let it go unless forced.

"Hans." Her eyes widened, brows arched then crashed down into a hard frown. "I despised you for what you did."

"As you should have. I'm sorry even now for pulling such a stupid prank." Leo pulled his hands free and held them out toward Roxie.

She noticed but didn't move to take his hands. "Why did you tell him I had the hots for him? I've never understood why you'd do such a thing when we were dating exclusively. Can you explain that?"

He meekly lowered his hands to his sides and took a deep breath. "Like I said, I was stupid. I'd overheard him saying he liked you and wished he had a chance with you. I knew he didn't, but I thought it would be funny to see what would happen." He dragged a hand through his hair and shook his head. "It never occurred to me he'd seriously try to steal you away from me."

She glared at him for several heated moments. "He sent me love notes for weeks. Popped up everywhere I went, asking for a date. Even to go to the senior prom I'd already said I go to with you. A movie. Biking. Anything."

Leo lowered his head to stare at the ground, bopped a piece of gravel into the underbrush with the toe of his shoe. "I did finally confess to him I'd lied about your feelings for him."

He didn't look up but pretended to be fascinated by the size and shape of the rocks at his feet. He didn't want to see the anger or disappointment in her eyes. Couldn't face her renewed dismay over his juvenile idiocy. He'd risked everything and nearly lost it all. Then he'd fled town before the prom and lost her anyway.

"Leo, look at me."

"I don't want to." He slowly shook his head and glanced away. "I was so stupid."

"Stop calling yourself stupid." She placed her fingers under his chin and eased his head up until he met her hard gaze. "I forgave you for the whole episode a long time ago. Ancient history now." She smiled softly at him as she lowered her hand.

He caught it and then reached for the other, waiting until she gave it to him. He peered into her eyes, searching for any hint of reproach or continued affront but saw only a calm acceptance and kindness. A spark of warmth lit his core, reviving a brief sense of inner strength before subsiding. She really had forgiven him for testing their relationship. "That's it!"

She startled, nearly pulling her hands free at his sudden exclamation. "What is?"

"The answer to the riddle's question." He chuckled and squeezed both hands with his. "I'm the 'one' who faked Hans' feelings as the 'other' and you are the 'third' who paid the price. So when the 'one' or rather me repented, then I received your forgiveness."

"Forgiveness. You're right." She pulled him in close to plant a kiss on his lips and he automatically embraced her as he always had.

He took his time and savored the sweet taste of her mouth under his, slipped his tongue inside to fully explore the familiar depths. Holding her again released all the sensations of their youth. The feel of her within his embrace, the brush of her hair across his bare arms as she moved within the circle of his strength. A soft moan vibrated against his chest as she snuggled closer, wrapped her arms around his back and clung to his shoulders. Gently, he eased them apart but only far enough to seek out her reaction. She opened her eyes to gaze into his, a slow smile gracing her lips.

"You haven't lost your touch." Roxie briefly pressed another kiss to his mouth. "I've missed you."

"Me, too." He'd resisted returning to the area, to her, for all the right reasons.

How could he come home without subjecting his carefully constructed life to analysis and criticism? He'd made his choice and therefore must act accordingly. His career waited for him in another city, another state, another world.

Yet he'd never felt any desire toward any other woman. The standard had been set by his love for the woman he held in a snug embrace. He'd met many beautiful and intelligent young ladies in his travels with the team and around Atlanta, but they didn't displace Roxie from the throne of his heart. No one could.

Yet it didn't change his reality. Until they finished the quest, he'd enjoy spending the little time they had together but then he'd have to return to his real life. The carefully constructed life he couldn't turn his back on. He didn't have another option. He had bills to pay, ball games to play, a team to support. Maybe even the World Series to pitch in if he could help his team win more games. All the hard-fought-for aspects of his adult life in the big city. He'd left small-town life far behind. Left all the people of his youth in the dust in order to become the man he intended.

So why did his heart ache at the mere thought of leaving her behind yet again?

Roxie gave him another light kiss. "We need to find the next charm now that we know the riddle's answer." She brought her hands around to press against his chest, separating them farther. "Where do you think it might be?"

Her lips tempted him but he saw determination in her eyes. The moment he might have kissed her in response passed in the blink of an eye and vanished. "When you forgave me, we saw a movie to make up."

"The theater. That's a likely place. We went there quite often." Roxie consulted her phone for the time and then huffed out a breath. "They don't open for a while yet."

"Good. I'm starving." Leo held out a hand and waited until Roxie put hers in his grasp. "Let's find a place to eat lunch on the way."

"Now who's always hungry?" She chortled as they walked hand in hand back to the parking lot.

Realizing his hunger extended farther afield than food, he strode in silence at her side for several minutes. He couldn't let his remembered feelings for her return let alone to grow into something more. If he had any hope of keeping his heart intact after he went back to the city, he must keep distance between them. Protect them both from a repeat of the former heart break that brought him to his knees. Must keep it light and friendly. As they rounded the last curve in the trail to reach the trailhead, he squeezed her fingers briefly.

"Race you to the car!" He dropped her hand and took off for his Corvette. Tagging the hood, he turned to catch her with both hands as she plowed into him. He steadied her, resisting the urge to pull her closer, continue the intimate moment of before. But he firmed his resolve to maintain space between them. "I won."

"No fair, you didn't give me warning." She pulled back slowly and brushed her ponytail off her shoulder with one hand. "I'd have beaten you otherwise."

He forced himself to let go, though his hands ached to cling to her sensual warmth. "No doubt. But now let's go find some food."

He opened the car door for her to slide inside, shutting away any lingering desire with a firm push of the door. As he started the engine, he had one goal above all others. He must be strong for them both or history might repeat itself.

Chapter Seven

O n their drive back to town, Leo had chosen a curious country diner to stop at for lunch. At least it seemed curious to Roxie's buzzing brain, thoughts swarming like a disturbed hornets' nest. Walking side-by-side with the man who caused said buzz, she could only marvel at his choice. They crossed the gravel parking lot toward the several steps up to a wraparound porch, where she spotted two rotund women chatting together. Dressed alike in below-the-knee khaki skirts and wildly flowered blouses. The pair turned as one to greet Roxie and Leo as they stopped in front of them.

"Welcome to Nicki's Cafe. I'm Shelly and this here is Shelia." Shelly, distinguished from her companion by her light blue hair and dark, laughing eyes, flapped a hand between them. "We're glad you all stopped in for a bite to eat."

"Go on in with you and Jeff will find ya a place." Not to be left out, Shelia made an exaggerated sweep of her arm to usher the new arrivals into the bustling restaurant behind the greeters. "Be sure to ask about the specials. Nicki's whipped up some fine offerings today."

"Thanks." Leo grasped Roxie's upper arm and propelled her past the overly cheerful women.

Inside, Roxie stopped by the hostess station, waiting for Jeff to arrive as promised. Leo released her arm and glanced around. The black-and-white checked floor made a perfect contrast to the red café curtains at the windows. Customers filled most every booth and table in sight, the aromas of burgers and fried onions wafting past Roxie's nose.

"I didn't realize how hungry I am." She inhaled the enticing smells, her mouth watering and her stomach grumbling in response.

"This must be Jeff." Leo tilted his head in the direction of a middle-aged man wearing dark blue trousers and a white shirt hurrying toward them with a clipboard in hand.

"How many?" He smiled at them, revealing a gold capped front tooth.

Soon Leo and Roxie held menus in a booth at the far reaches of the dining room. A slender young waitress in dark blue shorts and red tee shirt with the café logo on the back brought them their drinks and took their order. Roxie found herself across yet another table from Leo with nothing to do but look at him. Compare him with her memory of his younger self. The changes in him blended together into a more mature, more handsome man. One she couldn't stop looking at. But she could sense his inner defense in place against any feelings he might harbor towards her, let alone them.

Better to start a conversation than simply inspect every nuanced change in his expression, his appearance. "How did your father die? I don't think you mentioned the cause of death."

Homer King had been a larger-than-life kind of man. The spitting image of Leo except with a hardy laugh and not as muscular. Filled with a wicked sense of humor and passion for his work with the Order. He'd inspired everyone to strive to do better, accomplish as much as possible with the talents and skills each possessed. Expected everyone to do their absolute best. High standards to live up to. He'd been a second father to Roxie and her sisters after their own father had died. She'd lost touch with him after her mother died only because she'd been in such pain. Any connection to OWL would only stir up the anguish. So she'd put up her own defensive barriers. Merely speaking to him, anyone, at her mother's funeral had been supremely difficult.

"No, I didn't say how he died. It was sudden." Leo's eyes clouded briefly before he blinked and studied Roxie with a deep hurt simmering in them. "The death certificate lists ruptured brain aneurysm as the cause. The house cleaning crew found him when they arrived, apparently two days after he died."

"Oh, I'm so sorry. He was alone." Roxie reached across the table to clasp his hands. "You didn't have a chance to say goodbye."

"No." Anguish flashed across Leo's features as he continued to frown. "I came as soon as I could to see to the funeral arrangements."

"When will it be? I'd like to be there for you."

He turned his hand over to squeeze hers, his eyes haunted. "I'm sorry. The funeral was the morning of the day I came to the store."

She pulled her hands away and sat back in the chair, trying to comprehend the meaning of his words. "Why didn't you let us know? We loved your father. He was a huge part of our life growing up."

The picnics and hikes to discover as many types of birds or flowers they could find. Joint family dinners and birthday celebrations with balloons and candles on the cakes. Christmas evening bonfires with s'mores and ghost stories as they sat around the blaze. Quiet talks aside when she needed guidance from a father-figure. Homer wasn't blood but the very closest thing to it. Indeed, he'd served the role of father, of dad, to her. Tears rolled unheeded at the realization of the depth of hurt his loss created in her soul.

Leo pressed his lips together as he fished in his back pocket and then handed her a folded handkerchief. "The Order knew what he wanted and had already started putting the wheels in motion when I arrived. I merely had to sign some papers and then we had the funeral. I guess I was in shock and didn't think beyond what I had to deal with. I am deeply sorry, Roxie." He wiggled the fingers of his hand, palm up on the table.

"It's my fault, too." She mopped her face dry as she gazed at him for several seconds. "I distanced myself completely from the Order after Mom died. There didn't seem to be any reason to stay in touch."

"I get that. I didn't keep in contact with any of the other members after I left." He sat silently staring at her with a distant look in his eyes, his palm still ready and waiting for her to place her hand on top.

"Where is he buried?" She didn't take his hand, still a touch miffed and hurt by the oversight on both of their parts. But she couldn't ignore the invitation entirely either. "Can I at least say goodbye?"

"His letter of instruction spelled out he was to be cremated and then his ashes scattered up on the plateau." A gentle smile settled on Leo's lips even though his eyes turned serious. "I'm afraid he's mingling with the wind and soil now."

"On the plateau. Why didn't you say something while we were up at the park?" A lead weight rested in her heart, disappointment and pain at being denied closure with the man who had been so much a part of her childhood. She hadn't sought him out after her mother died but she never stopped caring about him. "I could have said something this morning."

"What would saying something do? Not even one of your spells could bring him back." Leo stirred his sweet tea with a straw bobbing in the icy fluid. "What's done is done."

"Bah." She crossed her arms, refusing to touch him when he held so little regard for her feelings. When she'd let her grief shield her too much from those she loved and cared for, to the point of being unavailable, inaccessible from such a momentous day as the memorial service for Homer King. "Of course I can't bring the dead back to life, nor would I want to. But I could have…asked the spirits to guide his journey to the other side. Told him how I felt, that I loved him. I'll miss him. His smile, his laugh, his advice. You don't understand, do you?"

"I said I'm sorry, Roxie." He took a long sip through the straw and then met her gaze with guarded eyes. "Coming back to this place, the people, all of the memories threw me for a huge loop and I don't think I've recovered from the crash landing yet."

He *had* suddenly lost his father. Had to face the many kindnesses and condolences while grieving and trying to process the immense hole in his life. No longer having any living parents to turn to for help, solace, unquestioning acceptance and love. She remembered when her mother had died without warning how long it took the three sisters to find their equilibrium, their footing, some sense of normalcy. The void left behind in their lives may slowly be filled but it would take a lot longer than three years. Homer King had only been dead for a month. Leo needed time and compassion not her piling on her own pain.

She needed to work on her quick temper. Too often she reacted without considering the other person's feelings. What emotions and distress they may be working through. She stifled a sigh at her lack of understanding. She, an empath, should feel their pain, confusion, uncertainty. Yet her temper often obscured and hid their emotions from her.

"I'm sorry, too." She unfolded her arms and clasped his hand. "I overreacted and shouldn't have unloaded on you like that."

"It's okay. I know the shock can be hard to grapple with." Leo squeezed her fingers and then pulled his hands free as the waitress delivered their sandwiches. The waitress made sure they had everything they needed and left. He poured a puddle of tomato catsup on his plate and dipped a fry before catching Roxie's attention again. "What happened with your mom? How did she die?"

The sudden shift in topic to her mother pulled her up short. Peggy had died suddenly, like his father. Not completely alone in the house but alone nonetheless. Tara had wanted to use her healing touch to treat their mother for a headache. But she had refused, saying the pain would go away on its own. When Tara had gone in to let her know about a special cake she'd made for her, she'd found her mother had passed away. The storm of grief coupled with the controlled chaos of planning her funeral, of handling the will and all that went with closing the estate, drew the sisters closer together than ever before. They'd grown to rely upon each other in every aspect of their lives.

Until Tara met Grant, and then Beth met Mitch, adding a new dimension to the strong bond between them. Roxie studied Leo for a long moment, wondering if he would eventually be in her life again or leave as he claimed. What man would she add to the family? If any. She had never found another man to love when he'd left the last time. She held out little hope for the future after he made good on his intent for a repeat performance. In the meantime, she'd strive to be pleasant but not share anything deeply personal. Not allow herself to become as attached as in the past. Keep her heart in one piece with any luck.

"Mom died in her sleep of an apparent heart attack." She grabbed her sweating glass and took a long sip of the sweet tea. Tried to wash away the sorrow lingering inside. The reverberating grief had mellowed to a soft throb in her core when she allowed herself to contemplate that dreadful span of time but it hadn't disappeared. "Tara found Mom when she went to wake her from a nap one evening."

"It's so hard losing a parent. I'm glad you have your sisters to help you through it." Leo tapped a finger on the table in a steady rhythm. "Sometimes I wish I hadn't been an only child. Then again, it would have complicated everything, I suppose. The big question for me now is what to do with the house. My childhood home."

Hope surged in Roxie's chest. An anchor for him to Roseville and his roots. "Are you thinking of moving into it?"

A quick shake of his head squashed the flare of hope. "I don't see how I could with my team so far away and playing all over. I suppose I'll have to clear it out, clean it up, and put it on the market."

The old house had lots of character. She'd visited a few times growing up. It's Victorian style suggesting a link to the historical nature of the county. Complete with a round room on one corner, turrets and fancy woodwork. She'd played Jumping Jibbitz and Mystical Mayhem with Leo on the wide verandah stretched across the back of the house, time flying by as they'd been absorbed in the intricate magical realms. The house overlooked a small pond with a diving board. Willows surrounded the water and reflected in its calm surface. They'd gone swimming in the cool water on hot days. Hiked the surrounding hills with eager strides, away from the knowing looks of his father. Swung on the porch swing with snow cones—hers, cherry with marshmallow cream, his, grape and lemon mixed together—from the passing truck playing enticing tunes as it plied its icy wares. So many good times centered on the enchanting place.

"That would be hard to do. Sell your childhood memories, I mean." Roxie lifted half of her chicken salad wrap and took a bite, letting the savory and sweet flavors engulf her senses.

"I'll always have the memories, just not all the stuff." Leo grabbed hold of his grilled chicken sandwich and bit into the stack of meat, cheese, and avocado.

She liked the way his mouth moved when he chewed and swallowed. Liked most everything about the man sitting yet again across the table from her. Memories of past meals shared over their entire lives flowed past her mind's eye. Everything from impromptu snacks on the porch to backpack picnics, and formal family holiday meals. Some of the most memorable being the ones they'd shared as young lovers out on a date. Sneaking nibbles off each other's' plates. Pushing bites of tater tots or pulled monkey bread into the other's mouth. Sucking a thick and frosty chocolate milkshake through two straws, a race to the bottom. So many fond and friendly meals. How many more to come? She hoped she wouldn't be able to count them on her fingers.

Once the quest ended with the last charm and the last spell read, he'd flee Roseville and her. Go back to his other life. The one he seemed to prefer.

Away from the small town where he and she had grown up together under the careful and loving guidance of their parents. Peggy and Homer worked alongside the other covens of witches of the circle to provide a safe and nurturing environment for a long time. Always comfortable in each other's presence. A sounding board for new ideas as the years went by. They'd worked together as easily as a well-oiled machine, anticipating needs and adjusting approaches in tandem. They made quite a pair, a couple of dedicated and sincere leaders for the circle. A sudden thought blossomed in her mind and she frowned as she tried to puzzle out an answer.

"What's up?" Leo poked some lettuce into the bun before taking another bite of sandwich. He quickly chewed and swallowed. "You look stunned."

"I just wondered why our parents never remarried after their spouses died." The weight of a frown pulled down on her brows as she squinted at him. Considered her suspicion from every angle but came to only one conclusion. "Do you think your dad and my mom liked each other?"

"I assume so since they worked together for so long." He bit into the chicken and chewed, drawing her attention to the tempting mouth in action. "Why?"

"Don't talk with your mouth full, silly. I can't understand you." She shook her head at him. "I mean, do you think they *liked* each other? You know, like we once did."

"Like us?" He paused in mid-chew and stared at her, his head slowly angling to one side. "Huh. Maybe."

"He came to my mother's funeral, did you know?" Roxie's thoughts turned inward, trying to recall what had bothered her about his presence at the sad occasion.

"No. I didn't talk to him very much."

"He said he came for my sake." She stared at Leo's face but saw only the inner image in her mind of Homer King hovering on the edges of the gathering at the memorial service held at the OWL headquarters Grand Hall.

Wearing his formal robes, Homer had presided over the affair in the somberly draped chamber. Intoned words of comfort and courage for those left behind after her mother's death left the members feeling bereft. He'd vowed to carry on as she had wanted until such time as new leaders were deemed necessary. Presumably after he died, which at the time she'd thought would be decades in the future. But after his eulogy to Peggy, he seemed to deflate, grow older before her eyes, as he'd stepped off the dais and moved slowly through the crowd. Wending his way to her side over a period of minutes where he'd really surprised her.

"At Mom's funeral, your dad said something rather odd to me." She laid her sandwich down and wiped her hands on a paper napkin. Shoved the wad under the edge of her plate as she brought her attention away from the memory to rest on Leo. "I haven't thought about it since but at the time it seemed very curious to me."

Leo hefted his sandwich as he considered her for several seconds. "What did he say?" He took a big bite and chewed thoroughly.

Roxie couldn't think about the long ago day while Leo somehow made chewing his food a turn-on, made her squirm in her seat, and long to draw his very mobile mouth to hers. Let him consume her as if she might taste as good. She shook herself and forced her gaze to stay on his eyes.

"Your dad said, and I'm paraphrasing, 'With Peggy's passing, the time of destiny draws nearer with each passing moment' but when I asked him what he meant he simply shook his head and walked away." She leaned forward, resting her hands on either side of her plate. "Do you think somehow he referred to this quest? Mom's note mentioned finding our destiny at the end."

"He obviously knew about the quest since he left the note and box for me to find." Leo swallowed and thankfully laid the last piece of sandwich on the plate. "Which means, we simply need to go find the next charm and wrap this up. Then we can get on with our destinies, whatever they may be."

"I'm not sure I want to know what kind of destiny the Order thinks awaits for us." Roxie clenched her hands into fists and laid them on her thighs. She'd made a good life for herself and didn't want anything mystical to be messing with it. "I like my life the way it is. I'm happy in Roseville and taking care of the simple needs of its people."

Catching up each morning with the daily lives of the townspeople who frequented the shop for coffee and a pastry, or to pick out a new book to learn something new. To linger a while and chat with the other people popping in for a few minutes' chat over hot tea and a bagel with cream cheese. Browsing the many stories and memoirs available to read. Picking out a gift for someone's birthday or graduation. All the little and big moments in a person's life to celebrate and revel in over the years. The joys and sorrows as well as the triumphs and challenges. She belonged right where she was. A place where she could help others reach their potential as well as to be part of a community, a large, boisterous, sometimes unruly but always supportive family.

Leo grunted at her claim of happiness but didn't outright dispute it. "I don't need some prophecy or spell to tell me where I belong." Leo scrabbled his napkin into a ball and laid it on his plate. "Your destiny may be in sleepy little Roseville tending to its pedantic flock. But mine waits in Georgia."

As much as she agreed with him about the slower pace of the small town, a part of her sensed their destiny had been decided for them long ago. As early as their childhood. Before they'd even met perhaps. Definitely something had changed the moment in the park when she'd pulled Leo to safety using her personal magic.

She'd felt the shift inside her when he stood holding her for so many minutes, stifling sobs of remembered fear of falling off the ledge to his death and the relief of being safe. Her own sense of power and accomplishment had been mitigated by the overwhelming joy of having him become part of her in a new and startling way. A way she'd never experienced before or with anyone else including her sisters. Something more had transpired she'd never put into words, nor tried to relay to anyone. For once in her life, words could not express the innate nature of the bond she sensed between them. A bond which had been tested to its utmost when he'd chosen a path away from home and her.

But destiny didn't change based on individual choices. No, the choices made simply wove a stronger tie to the inevitable. Provided the tools and skills necessary to make each capable of fulfilling his or her ultimate destiny.

Soon, though, they'd learn the true nature of their fate, one clue and one charm at a time. For now, she'd keep her own counsel and guard her fragile heart.

"We'll see in time. Speaking of which…" She checked the display on her phone and then started to gather her things. "The theater should be open by now. Let's go."

Neon lighting on the marquis of the Magnus Theater did far more than merely announce the show times and movies. As always, one classic movie and one new release title were advertised in black and white. The wraparound dark blue stripes evoked a flash flood of memories. So many recollections had been flushed into the open since Leo had returned to Roseville. Too many, perhaps. The Magnus had been a favorite hideout in his teens. Either with his goofy friends or with Roxie. Mostly with Roxie.

As they walked down the sidewalk toward the two-story white building, he fought to push the memories back into their cavern. Fought to not take her hand as habit clamored inside, making him flex his fingers when they neared one of two glass doors flanking the protruding ticket booth. He couldn't turn back the clock and start the painful journey all over again.

"We'll just slip inside and find the box and go on." He practically yanked open the door, holding it while Roxie hesitated.

"We don't need to buy a ticket?" She shot a worried glance at the woman in the booth, watching them.

"Not to look around the lobby." He waved her inside with his free hand. "Go on. Let's get this over with."

"If you say so." She strode inside but stopped a few feet from the door. "Wow."

Leo let the door bump closed behind him as he joined her. Gaped at the posh décor of the place he'd taken for granted in his youth, to the point of not actually seeing what surrounded him. "Yeah, wow."

The lobby of the Magnus vied in beauty with the big city cinemas. Red and white checkered floor stretched across the open space. A ticket taker stand stood in the center with drooping black ropes attached to silver poles at regular intervals stretched to either side. Large colorful posters advertising upcoming movies hung on the walls. The mouthwatering aroma of freshly popped popcorn and warm melted butter careened into his senses. At the back of the room were two doors leading to the two theaters. Leading into the darkened place where he'd once snuggled with Roxie on more than one occasion.

"It's like nothing has changed since the last time…" Roxie slowly spun in place, her jaw dropping open. "Not even the arcade cove."

Leo followed her gaze and laughed out loud. They'd taken to calling the tiny room off to one side the arcade cove because it only held two pinball games. They'd played the Star Wars pinball machine for hours at a stretch, taking turns on who held high score honors. When the owner switched the machine out for a soccer themed one, they'd both shrugged and walked away. What fun would it be to play that? No laser sword fights or Death Star to defeat.

"I feel like I've walked into the Twilight Zone." He didn't want nor need to take another trip back in time. He heard faint pounding on the mental door to events and happenings of his past, all eager to be freed. Humming to himself, he silenced the inner distraction. "Let's do this."

"Where do you want to start?" She looked about and then back at him. "The arcade?"

"Good idea. We spent a lot of time in there." He started across the floor, Roxie alongside. "They still have the sharpshooter game."

Dual air rifle handles poked from the front of the machine so two players could shoot at the same time. Competing for bragging rights with each shot at the electronic target. Leo had always won when he played against Roxie but he still wondered if she'd let him. He never believed she wasn't adept at most everything she tried. Perfect, in fact.

"Maybe over here? Give me your hand." Roxie eased to the side of the machine pressed against the wall. She reached in with their joined hands to feel alongside the metal. After several seconds, she shook her head and withdrew their hands. "Where else?"

Leo worked his mouth to one side, pondering other options as he perused the small alcove. "The other machine, maybe?"

"We can try." She brushed past him, intent on crossing the tiny space, her enticing bum grazing his thigh in the process.

He sucked in air, striving for calm. Swallowed hard as he mentally squared his shoulders. He must get a grip on himself. Following her, he caught up in time for her to snatch his hand and repeat the search on the other side of the machine. In doing so, he bumped into her back as she maneuvered his hand in front of her. He braced against the game and held still for the torture of three seconds, so close to her he could hear her mutterings as she felt around, smelled her sweet perfume. When she straightened, she banged the back of her head into his nose.

"Ow." Leo jerked back, freeing his hand and putting a few feet between them to gingerly touch his nose to see if she'd broken it.

"Sorry." She quickly closed in to peer at him as she lay a cautious hand on his arm. "Are you okay?"

"It's not broken. Is it bleeding?" He felt underneath his nose and then inspected his fingers. No red. "Don't do that again, okay?"

"I said I'm sorry. Here, let me make it all better." She leaned forward and brushed a butterfly kiss over his nose before crossing her arms as her concern morphed into a laugh. "Maybe I should wear a 'keep back 100 yards' sign as fair warning."

He opened his mouth to reply then snapped it shut before the revealing words could escape. The words telling her he didn't want to be so far away ever again. Which, of course, was ridiculous and impossible, to boot.

"Maybe you should." He forced a laugh to cover his agitation. "Where else do you think we should look?"

Roxie smiled at someone behind Leo as she dropped her hands to her sides. "We have company."

Leo shifted so he could see the stern manager halt in front of them. Old enough to be Leo's father but without the charismatic power Homer King had possessed. The wiry man with equally wiry gray hair glanced at both of them with a slight frown and then forced a professional yet insincere smile onto his lips.

"What do you think you're doing?" His deep, gravelly voice grated on Leo's nerves.

"Nothing. Just looking around." Leo matched the man's smile with one of his own. No way would he share their true purpose for returning to the nostalgic old theater.

"Do you have tickets?" The manager raised one brow as he stared at Leo.

"No, sir." Leo's smile withered and fell away. "Like I said, we simply wanted to see the lobby again."

"We haven't been here in a very long time." Roxie smiled, a much more sincere and thus believable friendly expression than either of the two men had attempted. "Nothing's changed."

"One thing has for certain." The man's pale blue eyes glinted in the light shining from the bright chandeliers. "You have to buy a movie ticket before you come into the lobby. This isn't a sightseeing stop on some tour."

"We only need a few minutes and we'll be out of here." Leo cut a glance at Roxie, who nodded.

"Absolutely."

"Either buy tickets to watch a movie or leave. Those are your options." The manager crossed his arms over his narrow, self-righteous chest, his Adam's apple prominently sliding up and down his scrawny throat. "No exceptions."

"But—" Leo objected with his entire being. He couldn't do it. Even if his libido wanted him to.

Sit in a darkened theater with Roxie at his side. Within reach of draping his arm around her, her head resting on his shoulder. Or playing thumb wars while they watched the movie. Sharing buttered popcorn out of a large tub between them, their fingers brushing when they both reached in at the same time. Like all the previous times they'd enjoyed being together.

"No exceptions." The manager shook his head. "Your choice."

The charm hid somewhere within the walls of the theater. He sensed they were close, a niggling in his core like he hadn't felt in a long time. He couldn't leave without the charm. Leo clenched his jaw as he noticed Roxie's curt nod indicating they should do as the manager insisted. If she could do it, then he'd have to man up. Be a true gentleman and keep his hands to himself. No matter what. If possible…

"Very well. I'll go buy them." He dragged in a long breath and then met Roxie's questioning gaze. "Only You or the horror flick?"

He hoped she wouldn't choose the classic film they'd watched together years before. A romantic comedy about fortune telling, fate, deceit, and finding true love. Too much like the twisting turns of their own relationship. Better to watch anything else than to sit through echoes of the mistakes and the memories they'd made.

"Horror." Roxie grinned at him, her luscious lips calling to him.

He blew out his held breath and inwardly rejoiced at her selection. No touching sentiment to wade through. Nothing to make him think more deeply or, worse, feel more deeply about who they might have been together as a couple.

With a nod, he spun around and hurried back outside to the ticket booth. Away from her alluring lips. He could do it. Without succumbing to the tantalizing woman who exemplified his ideal mate. His perfect woman.

Then she smiled her come-hither smile at him when he approached her in the lobby, waiting with the young ticket taker guy and the pleased manager. An invitation as comfortable as the memories flooding through the now unlocked, wide open door in his mind.

He braced himself mentally as he carried the tub of popcorn in one arm and walked with her toward the theater door. She carried both cups of soda. Leo glanced over his shoulder to see the manager watching him with a smile of triumph. Leo turned back around, met Roxie's guarded gaze, and pulled open the door to the theater. He could do this. He must.

Maybe.

Chapter Eight

The theater was a ghost town. Roxie suggested two seats in the center section toward the back of the theater. In case anyone else sauntered in later. Better to know who else she might know in the audience. Who might spread false rumors about her and Leo getting back together. Because, clearly, if there was one thing Leo had made plain it was his desire to leave. The town and her. She plunked down in a seat and then settled the cups into holders. Scanned the empty seats. Hoped somebody would join them to obliterate the intimacy of the private setting.

The previews started as they munched on popcorn. She timed it so she picked up the fluffy white kernels when his hand was nowhere near. No accidental touching. Even if she leaned away from him in her seat, she could enjoy the secret thrill of sitting with him, ready to watch a movie together for the first time in too many years. She longed to snuggle up to him as in days of old, resting her head on his brushed flannel shoulder, feeling his breath in her hair, but refrained. Still, being with him again made her inner self sing with joy.

"Sorry about this." Leo grabbed a handful of popcorn and started shoving it into his mouth a few pieces at a time.

Did he suspect her secret? Hopefully not. She sipped her lemon-lime beverage while he grabbed another handful of popcorn. Then risked reaching into the tub herself. "Just means it will take longer to find the charm."

"We could walk out at any time and resume our search." He crunched on another mouthful for a moment then swallowed. "He couldn't stop us."

Her pleasure chilled with his suggestion. True, they could. She needed to convince him to stay. For a while at least. So she could savor the new memory after he left. After her life returned to its usual routine and the excitement of the quest ended.

"We should stay for a while." She lifted another handful of popcorn out of the tub. "Until the manager loses interest in our actions."

"Good point." He sucked on the straw in his cup, pulling root beer into his mouth. "I haven't seen this movie. Have you?"

"No, All the more reason we should watch it." She regarded him as the previews flashed and blared on the screen. "I hope it's not too scary."

His eyes widened as he stared at her for several seconds. "It's been a long time since we've seen a scary movie together."

A hint of a smile quirked his lips as her neck and then her cheeks warmed. She'd forgotten. How *could* she have forgotten how she'd grab hold of his powerful and protective arm when she was scared by the movies they watched? He remembered and obviously liked that she'd done so. Her macho caveman guy. All about protecting his frail lady from big bad bogeymen. She nearly burst out laughing but pressed her lips together and his gaze dropped to her mouth then met her eyes again. Hinting at a mutual desire. She swallowed, blinked away the intimate thought.

"It's starting." She inclined her head at the screen, relieved the start of the feature ended the awkward moment.

She fell silent as the opening scenes captured her attention. A few minutes into the movie, a flurry of motion at the side entrance interrupted the action for Roxie. An older couple made their way slowly to seats a few rows in front of her and Leo. The woman even wore pin curls, a style Roxie hadn't seen in a long time. The man grunted as he adjusted his jacket and laid his hat on the armrest of the next chair. At least she had a chaperone of sorts. Finally, they fell silent and still and Roxie could slide back into the story playing on the big screen.

She jumped at one particular point in the movie and surprised them both when she reflexively grabbed hold of his forearm. She jerked her hand away and clasped both together in her lap. He chuckled softly for a moment then smiled at her. Relaxed, relieved he hadn't overreacted to her slip up. She watched the movie, letting the story carry her away. Until another startling scene made her grab his arm again.

"Sorry." She shrugged it off, hoping he'd do likewise.

With only a slight inclination of his head and a comforting smile, he enveloped her hand in his and turned his attention back to the movie.

The strong, warm hand provided her with an anchor as the story unfolded. When Leo shifted to put his arm around her shoulders, she melted against him with relief. She'd not say no to reliving their past. Adding to the cache of memories of being with him she'd carry inside forever. As the credits played and the lights came up, she moved to sit up straight. The other couple made a production of rising and gathering their trash before shuffling out of the theater. All the while, Leo held her in his one-arm embrace. Eventually drawing her gaze to his questioning one.

"Roxie…" He stared into her eyes then at her mouth before meeting her hopeful gaze. "May I?"

Without any doubt in the whole wide world. She couldn't say no to such a magnificent idea. He shifted around enough so there lips could meet. She closed her eyes as a rush of sensation and happiness tumbled inside. Hope bursting into her soul as he deepened the kiss, exploring and delving into her mouth. The electrical storm of his kiss zipping along her veins and zapping into her heart. Restarting the love for him she couldn't deny any longer. She succumbed to the deliciousness of his mouth on hers, her heart his forever. No matter what happened next.

The lobby seemed garishly bright when Leo followed Roxie out of the theater. A quick search of the room allowed him to relax his guard. Only the old married couple fastening their jackets off to one side. The man perused the lobby, meeting Leo's curious gaze for an instant. Then he went back to watching his lady fumbling with the zipper on her pea green jacket. The manager was nowhere in sight but he could pop up at any moment. If they worked quickly, they might locate the hidden box and leave before he had to confront the man again.

Then, after all the drama of the day had ended, he'd find a solitary place where he could process the mind-blowing kiss he'd shared with Roxie in the theater. Maybe out in the Golden house backyard by the fire pit, a glass of whiskey to settle his rampant libido. His fingertips still tingled from the connection between them he'd reignited when he wrapped his arm about her shoulders. Caved to the need to touch her. Hold her. Indeed, his whole body seemed more alive, more vital. He thought he'd moved on. Moved away to put the past behind. The more time he spent with Roxie the more he wanted to be with her. The more his entire body remembered how linked they used to be. How when they were apart, whether separated by a few miles or by states, he'd been half a person. Coming back meant he'd found his whole self again. Unacceptable. But true.

Despite his misgivings, or maybe because he felt bereft without touching her, Leo took Roxie's hand and briefly squeezed her fingers. "Let's find this thing."

"If we only knew where to look." She nodded and scanned the cheery lobby. "Somewhere around the concessions?"

"Worth a shot." He kept hold of her hand as they crossed the floor to investigate possible hiding places. After all, she'd taken his hand to poke around in one place and another. Why not maintain the contact?

After trying several small gaps and even behind the large silver container of paper wrapped straws, he sighed with frustration. "Where else?"

"The ticket booth?" She shot a frown his way and then shrugged. "It's been around forever."

The older woman in the green jacket moved suddenly from where she stood by the concessions. Pressed her bejeweled hand to the base of her throat, sparkling under the fluorescent lighting. She smiled and tilted her head toward the front door and the booth outside. Leo pointed at the door and she nodded once. Then the couple vanished.

Startled, Leo searched the lobby with quick, frantic glances. He and Roxie were alone in the space. Odd. Where was the ticket lady? The manager? Then his tumbling gut told him. Magic at work. The woman had indicated the ticket booth. He pulled on Roxie's hand to draw her along as he hurried outside to search for cubbyholes and hiding places around the thankfully empty booth. "I think it might be out here."

In the glass wall of the booth was a small gap above a shallow metal rectangular well. Only enough room to exchange money and tickets. Not enough to let people on the outside mess with the ticket seller. Peering closely, he could see the entire basin clearly. The dish looked empty.

"I don't see any other possibility." She squeezed his hand and then walked their fingers into the narrow slot to slide them around the edges of the shallow metal well. First the left side, then the back, and across to the right side. Where she paused. "Wait."

"I feel it, too." A flat rectangle of a box attached to the right wall. "I can't see it, but something is there."

"Pry off the front of the box while I hold the back steady." She glanced up and then back at Leo. "Hurry. The ticket lady. She's coming."

Sliding a finger under the edge, he pried it away and then grabbed the invisible object and pulled it free. Dropping it onto his palm, surprise and disbelief shivered through him as it turned into a silver box. Peggy's magic proved powerful and sophisticated beyond his imagination.

"Hey! What are you two doing there?" The matronly woman charged with the sale of tickets trundled up with a disapproving frown.

"We're just leaving. Thanks." Roxie gave the woman a little wave and then grabbed Leo's elbow to usher him down the sidewalk toward where the car was parked under a shade tree. By the time they reached the vehicle, they were both laughing with relief and success.

Like the spring day they'd gone hiking after he'd finally earned his full driving privileges. He'd driven them out to hike at the Walls of Jericho outside of Scottsboro, Alabama. He'd heard it was a short, beautiful hike. Only about six miles with gorgeous views and even a waterfall to reward their effort. They'd filled a backpack with bottles of water and some energy bars. He'd figured they'd be gone several hours so wouldn't need more provisions. He'd figured wrong.

The hike down into the valley went smoothly as they wended among mature trees. The trail twisted and turned down the steep side, finally leveling out as they crossed a sturdy tree bridge over a rushing creek. Birds darted among the upper branches of the trees while a cluster of colorful butterflies fluttered about at the side of the bridge. He'd paused long enough to point out the bluebells scattered over the nearby hillside, their purplish blooms stunning against the green and brown background of the forest floor.

They'd hiked on to see the rushing waterfall, replete with rainwater from recent spring dousings. They'd had the trail pretty much to themselves due to the cool temperatures and the threat of flooding from the rains. Being young, strong, and somewhat stupid, they'd ignored the warnings and ventured forth. Only when they turned around to head back out and up to the parking lot, did he realize how ill prepared they were. After they'd passed the creek, the water level had not only risen but accelerated its flow. Brushing the bottom of the tree trunk, sometimes splashing onto the bark, making crossing the bridge tricky to not slip off and downstream.

Then they'd started the climb up the steep side they'd easily almost ran down. Gravity worked against them as they struggled up and up the twisting, rock-strewn, sometimes muddy trail. The trail may have only been six miles long but he hadn't realized the return trip was mostly all uphill. Pausing frequently to let his racing heart calm, he led Roxie slowly back to where his old jalopy waited for them. Never had he been so glad to flop onto the seat of his car. After they'd drank the last of their water and commiserated on aching calves and thighs, they'd laughed at their own stupidity but also their success. They'd done it. Hiked the Walls of Jericho and lived to tell the tale. After overcoming such a challenge, he'd believed together they could handle anything.

He stared at the plain silver box on his palm. Now they had another ongoing challenge to overcome. One requiring both brains and an emotional connection in a far more intimate fashion than they'd ever before encountered.

Before fastening his seatbelt, Leo held out the box to Roxie. "Open it. Let's see where we're off to next."

"Could be most anywhere, couldn't it?" She removed the lid, placing it on the dashboard, then lifted a gold charm to show him. "Like we thought, comedy and tragedy masks represent the theater. One of our favorite haunts."

"Your mom is sending us to places where we have to relive important moments in our past." The woman sure knew more about their relationship than he'd realized at the time. "Is there another clue?"

"Of course. Let me attach the charm and then I'll see what it says." She tapped the charm to the bracelet. Then again. Nothing happened. "Odd. It won't go on."

"You must not be doing it right." Leo held out his hand. "Give it to me."

"It worked for you, why won't it work for me?" She tapped the charm to the links but no flare or melding of the link to the charm followed. "It's not doing anything."

"Let me try." He left his palm open, inviting her to lay the charm on it.

"Fine. See if you can put it on and then I'll read the next clue." Roxie dropped the charm onto his hand and then held out her left wrist.

Leo gingerly lifted the pair of masks and held it close to the bracelet. As before, as soon as the small loop fastened itself to the bracelet, the jewelry glowed bright—brighter than last time—for only a moment and then faded. They'd found four of the six charms. How much brighter would the thing glow when all the charms were in place? What exactly would happen when the quest ended and they read the final spell? Questions he wasn't sure he wanted to know the answers to but they would find out anyway.

"Should I be upset that it wouldn't go on for me?" Roxie pouted at the dangling charm, nudging it with her forefinger.

He thought about it for several seconds before he realized what had been missing. "No, I think it's yet another aspect of us having to work together. If you'd even been able to go find all the charms on your own, you wouldn't have been able to collect them on the bracelet without me."

"So she thought of everything. Why am I not surprised." Roxie unfolded the slip of gold paper and skimmed its contents. "This is interesting… Ready?"

"With bated breath. Just read it, please."

"Impatient, are we? Okay, okay. I'll read it." She cleared her throat dramatically. "Ahem."

What flies straight
Aiming for the heart
Striking true
Yet pierces no flesh?

"What the hell does that mean?" Leo chuckled without any shred of humor.

"I have no idea." Roxie stared at the paper, a frown weighing down her brows. "What strikes without piercing flesh?" Her phone rang and she dropped the paper into her lap to put her cousin on speaker. "Hey, Paulette. What's up?"

"We're putting together an impromptu family dinner. I needed to cook but I made enough to feed an army and it'll be ready soon. Can you be here in 30 minutes?"

"Wow, that's fast. I don't know…" Roxie raised a brow at Leo who nodded his enthusiasm. She smiled at his eagerness. "Looks like Leo's as hungry as I am. So sure. We'll be there."

"Great. I'll tell the others you're on your way."

"Maybe you all can help Leo and me solve the next riddle in our quest." She picked up the slip to stare at it as she talked. "We don't understand what Mom meant by it."

Paulette chuckled on the line. "We can try. See you soon."

Roxie ended the call and put the phone back in her bag along with the paper and box. Then she turned to peer at Leo. "You okay?"

He started the car and then clicked his seatbelt home. "As good as I can be."

He wouldn't tell her the truth. The deep concern about the disappearing duo in the lobby. Had they confirmed Roxie's guess about the location or pointed them in the same direction to begin with? He knew magic played a role but couldn't determine in what way. He hadn't been contemplating mystical or magical elements in a long time since he'd had to make do without. Recent occurrences had him second-guessing everything. Not simply the magic abounding.

In addition to the mysterious appearance of the older pair and the unknown properties of the charm bracelet, his heart twisted and turned in anguish, torn by conflicting desires. Wanting to continue his burgeoning career as a baseball pitcher. Wanting to prove he could be not only an adequate but a great player even without his powers. Wanting—no, *needing* to be with Roxie.

Needing time to sort out his emotions. Needing to decide on his future. But most of all, needing to find a way forward which wouldn't ultimately hurt the very woman he finally had to admit to himself he loved.

The conflict inside made him out of sorts, grumpy, and craving time to himself. Time to think. But how, when Roxie insisted they stay close together? He drove on toward the plantation wishing he could be anywhere else.

Chapter Nine

$\mathscr{A}$ fire snapped and crackled in the double parlor at Twin Oaks, a cheery welcome on a mild fall day. Roxie shifted to watch Leo staring out the front window, legs braced and arms crossed. Ever since they'd arrived, he'd withdrawn into himself. Brooding and distant. Reminding her of the days before he left for other parts so many years ago. She sucked on her lower lip for a moment and then studied the fragrant fire. The temps remained in the seventies during the day, so the fire served more as decoration than a source of warmth. Useless but pretty. Or pretty useless. Much like she felt at the moment.

Meredith occupied the love seat, using a cinnamon stick to stir the steaming mug of apple cider in her hand. The distant sound of Paulette moving about the kitchen vied with the stereo playing something instrumental in the background. Tara reclined on the other love seat, tapping one manicured finger on her knee in time to the music. A peaceful gathering of the women in the family. Except…

"Where's Beth?" Roxie frowned as she crossed her ankles.

"Not coming. She and Mitch apparently had a bit of a tiff this morning while you and Leo were out making googly eyes at each other." Meredith smirked lovingly at Roxie. Then gripped the flowered mug with both hands as a light frown wrinkled her forehead. "Something about whether to go on a honeymoon, I think."

"First I've heard about a honeymoon." Roxie steepled her fingers in front of her chest, tapping each fingertip in sequence as she pondered the underpinnings of the argument. "Where are they thinking of going? I haven't heard Beth mention any destinations. Have you?"

Meredith shook her head slowly. "Not where, but whether. He says yes, she says no."

"I see. That is a disagreement." Roxie pursed her lips and then sank back against the seat. "They've been having more and more head-buttings of late."

She smothered a sigh as she recalled the litany of arguments between the two. She didn't doubt they loved each other. They'd proven so to themselves and everyone around them. So why the dissent? The differing approaches to almost every piece of the wedding planning puzzle? Invitations. Attire. Cake. Now honeymoon. She sensed something amiss but couldn't put her finger on the root cause.

"I'm sure they'll work it out." Meredith released the mug to wave one hand in the air. "Pre-wedding jitters most likely."

"I hope you're right. They belong together." Roxie lowered her hands to rest in her lap. "They really need to listen to each other more."

Paulette broke out into song in the kitchen, belting out the chorus to "I Will Survive" as footsteps sounded in the hallway. Roxie glanced to the wide doorway in time to see Max stride into view. Meredith had scored big when she'd fallen for the big, lovable lawyer. They made a perfect couple, balancing each other's strengths and bolstering each other's weaknesses. Together they could accomplish anything, all with love and trust between them.

Max sauntered into the parlor and sank onto the seat beside Meredith, aiming an inquiring grin at Roxie. "How did your search go?"

"Found another charm at the Magnus and a curious riddle." Roxie patted the bag beside her on the sofa. "No idea what it means, but a clue."

Leo glanced over his shoulder at her, his eyes dark and mysterious. He looked about to speak but then stared out the window again.

What was he thinking? Or feeling? They'd had one intense moment together followed by the discovery of the mask charm. Two positives to her mind. But then all the way back to the plantation, he'd grown quieter until he'd fallen as silent as a mute person. What was playing in his head? She wracked her memory, searching for something she might have said to flip a switch in his brain. Changed him from being open, holding her hand, even going so far as to kiss her like he'd been drowning with her, to the silent giant at the window. She must have said the wrong thing, sent the wrong vibe, or made the wrong move.

The idea of second guessing her every decision was a new one for Roxie. She typically moved forward with confidence in her decisions and knowing she'd said the right thing. Or the closest thing to it. She understood the power of words. The power of the proper names for both people and things. Avoided misusing words or misstating her position. Something had gone wrong.

"Okay, gang. It's almost ready." Paulette sashayed into the parlor, a huge smile on her face. "My world-famous ground beef stroganoff over delectable egg noodles, with an amazingly fresh tossed salad on the side."

"Sounds okay." Max nodded at her, a sly grin on his lips. "Did you order in?"

Paulette tapped his shoulder in mock hurt. "No, I didn't. How dare you?"

"Ouch." Max chuckled as he exaggeratedly rubbed his shoulder, pretending she'd injured him. "You win."

"You two stop." Meredith grinned as she shook her head at the two of them. "Always kidding around."

Paulette aimed laughing eyes at Roxie and then sobered. "So how did the quest go today? Did you find a charm?"

"Yes, out at the state park this morning, and that one led to one at the Magnus Theater."

"Two in one day?" Tara's hand stilled on her leg. "That was fast."

Roxie looked around at the gaping faces. "What? We have to solve this quickly so Leo can go home where he wants to be."

Not where she wanted him to go. But when you love someone you do what makes them happy. If Leo would be happier in Atlanta, then she'd do all in her power to help him find his way there as soon as possible. Even if it shattered her heart in the process. She'd recover. She'd done it before. She could do it again.

Meredith squinted at her but refrained from speaking. Her expression, though, shouted her doubts. She glanced from Roxie to Leo and then back to Roxie with arched brows. Roxie tilted her head briefly, not wanting to put her thoughts into words with Leo's stiff back a barrier to his feelings. Meredith firmed her lips, understanding Roxie's silent warning to not ask.

"So what's the new riddle?" Paulette crossed to sit with Roxie on the matching loveseat. "Can I see? I'm good at solving them."

Roxie unzipped the pouch and retrieved the gold slip to present to Paulette. "Read it out loud. The more brains the better."

Paulette scanned the paper and then read the four lines.

What flies straight
Aiming for the heart
Striking true
Yet pierces no flesh?

"Interesting. Let's see..." Max aimed twinkling eyes at her, though the rest of his expression remained stoic and somber. "The first line could be a bird, or a plane, or—"

"Do *not* say Superman." Meredith smacked his thigh with a light hand. "This is no laughing matter."

"Why not? I think Peggy Golden wanted them to have some fun." Max leaned slightly away so he could peer closely at his wife. "Together again."

Leo grunted but otherwise didn't engage in the conversation. He remained staring out the window even though he apparently listened to the chatter behind him. Roxie wished he'd join them rather than holding himself apart. Then maybe she could understand where his thoughts took him. Some deep dark well? A cold distant forest? Either way, she couldn't reach him.

"Yeah, why is it serious?" Paulette studied Meredith for several seconds.

"From what I've uncovered about quest spells, and yes I did some research on them." Meredith glared at her husband's mock surprised face and then smiled. "I know how to do an Internet search for pity's sake. Anyway, if it's not completed according to the rules of the spell, dire consequences will fall upon those enchanted."

Roxie nodded slowly, her heart quaking. "My mother's powers exceeded the average witch in the Order. She was Supreme Priestess for good reason. I can only imagine what those consequences might be."

"On that cheerful note, let's continue this discussion over dinner before it gets cold." Paulette pushed to her feet and started herding everyone out of the parlor and into the dining room down the hall. "You, too, Leo."

At mention of his name, he slowly turned and trailed after the group. Roxie glanced back at him, trying to catch his eye without success. If she could see into his eyes, maybe she could figure out what troubled him. She reached out with her mind, her heart, trying to ascertain more about his emotional state. She detected a murkiness, an indistinct thick cloud of emotions. Turmoil and resistance. She pulled back her probing, suddenly aware of how close to giving up on everything he seemed to be. She turned away from studying him to continue slowly down the hall after the others.

Soon everyone had steaming plates of stroganoff and a bowl of fresh greens, cucumbers, red bell pepper, and tomato salad. Conversation dwindled to "pass the pepper" or "this is delicious" or low murmurings of approval.

After a few minutes, Max drew Leo's attention with a hand laid on the table. "I was wondering, why did you decide to leave the area? What drew you to Georgia?"

Roxie chewed quietly, curious as to how Leo would answer.

"You really want to know?" Leo blinked twice before glancing to Roxie for a long moment. Then he met Max's gaze again with a grimace. "I'd always dreamed of playing in the major leagues. After I lost my...or rather, after I was punished, and Roxie and I broke up, there was nothing left for me here."

"Punished?" Paulette speared a piece of tomato and held it poised to eat. "For what?"

Again, Leo shot a look at Roxie before answering. "The truth?"

"Of course." Paulette chewed as she waited for his response.

"I used to be a warlock until I was accused and punished for abusing my powers. Then Peggy Golden, at my dad's request, bound my powers so I could no longer use them."

"What did you do to make them punish you?" Meredith laid her fork on her plate, a prepared bite of creamy beef ignored.

"Nothing really." Leo played with his fork, spinning it slowly in his long fingers.

Roxie contemplated the downward eyes, the tension in his shoulders. She reached out with her mind to feel what he felt and then pulled back. Hurt and shame warred inside although his face showed defiance in the set jaw and slight frown. He might want the world to believe he didn't regret his actions, but he most definitely felt embarrassed and defensive about what he did. Despite the hurt it might cause, telling the truth was the only way he could move on.

"I can tell you that." Roxie fisted her hands on either side of her plate.

"You tattled to your mother six years ago, so why not now?" Leo muttered.

Stung, Roxie stared at him. "It was the right thing to do, and you know it."

He met her gaze, blasted her with the hurt and disappointment shining in his eyes. "Go on, then."

She'd been so proud of him, for him, when he told her he'd made the varsity baseball team. Then he had to ruin the moment by bragging about how he'd used his powers to encourage the coach to see how much better he was than the other pitchers during the tryouts. Used his abilities for his own benefit, a taboo act according to the governance of the Order. She'd urged him to do the right thing then, to decline the team position. When he refused, she'd wrestled with her conscience but ultimately, reluctantly, had gone to her mother.

"Leo used his powers for self-gain, a cardinal sin among the members of OWL." Roxie's pulse beat in her ears as she glanced around the table. "When he wouldn't make it right, his dad, as Supreme Priest, asked my mother to do the honors of binding his powers until he proved himself mature enough to possess them."

"Was it painful?" Max scooped a bite onto his fork and ate it, chewing slowly.

"Yes." Leo's jaw tensed and a vein stood out in stark relief on his neck.

Roxie would never forget that horrible day in the living room of her home. The torture he'd endured in the process of restricting his powers. Her mother had seemed impervious to the pain he collapsed under, but later Roxie heard her crying in her bedroom. At that moment, the depth of anguish her mother suffered on his behalf became clear.

"You don't know this, but what my mother did hurt her nearly as much as you." She laid her fork down, her appetite gone. "It broke her heart to punish you knowing how close we were."

"Honestly? I doubt it."

"If you hadn't lied about what you did, the punishment wouldn't have been so bad." Roxie reached out a hand on the table, stretched toward where Leo sat across from her.

Max snapped his fingers as his eyes widened and a smile flashed onto his lips. "That's it!"

Startled, Roxie stared at him. "What?"

"The answer to the riddle. It's honesty." He looked from one to another, nodding furiously. "You said it yourself, if he'd been honest and hadn't lied."

"Honesty flies straight to the heart without piercing flesh." Roxie stared at Leo and nodded. "Which means we need to go back to where you weren't honest."

"Which is where, exactly?" Leo braced his hands on the edge of the table. Lifted his chin as worry clouded his eyes.

"You know where. The ball diamond at the high school." Roxie pressed her lips together as an array of reactions swept across Leo's features. Shock. Dismay. Anger.

"Never." He pushed back from the table and slowly stood. "I will never step foot on those grounds again."

"You might not like it, but you have to." Roxie shrugged as she willed him to sit back down and be a man about the situation. "The quest—"

"Be damned!" Leo shoved his chair in, gripping the back with one hand to rock it to and fro in an even rhythm. "Nothing and nobody will make me go there."

"Leo, be reasonable." Roxie stood, putting herself on more even footing with the glowering man. A quick assessment of the expectant faces around the table told her everyone held their collective breath as to what would happen next. She pressed her fingertips onto the table as she met his angry gaze. "That was a long time ago. You have to let it go. Now, please. Sit down and finish your dinner."

"Let it go?" Leo straightened his spine, releasing the chair to teeter and then settle into place. "You may have forgotten but I live with the reality of the consequences of your mother's actions every damn day of my life."

If they were cartoon characters, billowing steam would be jetting from each ear, he was so furious. She needed to calm him down before he did something unthinkable. He'd promised to see the quest through, but what if he did indeed let his inner turmoil take over? She shivered, not wanting to discover what consequences her mother may have in store for them if they failed.

Roxie moved around the end of the table to cautiously approach Leo, rigid as an iron bar. She reached out, intending to clasp his hand or his arm, but he pulled away. Clenching her fist loosely, she lowered her hand. "You agreed to finish this."

"I've changed my mind." His dark, angry eyes glared at her before he shook his head once. "I can't do this."

"You must. We must. Together."

"No, we don't." He pivoted and marched out of the room, down the hall, and soon she could hear footsteps on the stairs.

Roxie dragged in a calming breath and released it to the count of five. He'd fled upstairs to his guest room. Hopefully, he'd spend some time fuming and then realize he had no other option. She headed back to her chair and flopped onto the seat to scan the astonished faces of Paulette, Meredith, and Max.

"Well, that was unexpected." Paulette picked up her fork and resumed eating. "I guess he needed to chill for a bit."

"Should I go after him?" Max shifted, ready to follow through on his offer, but Roxie shook her head at him until he relaxed.

"Hopefully, he'll come around soon." Roxie glanced at the ceiling, wondering what he was doing. "We'll get back at it tomorrow after he realizes we have no choice but to go to the school."

Thundering footfalls on the stairs announced Leo returning. Instead of seeing him coming into the parlor, the front door opened and slammed shut. Roxie jumped to her feet, but hesitated to go after him. He was a grown man. If he needed some time to sort through his feelings, then she'd have to give it to him. But, oh, she'd rather race after him and make him understand. Maybe he merely stepped outside to cool down, sitting on the big front porch watching the ducks on the lake.

"Roxie, your bracelet…"

The concern quavering Meredith's voice made Roxie look down at her wrist. Alarm flashed through her. The bracelet glowed against her skin, brighter and brighter.

"I don't understand." She fingered the slender chain,

noting with growing concern how it cooled and then turned to ice around her wrist. "It's freezing."

"Take it off." Meredith pushed her chair back to rush to Roxie's side.

Roxie fumbled with the catch but it wouldn't release. "I can't."

"Let me try." Meredith attempted to unfasten the small clasp but shook her head. "It won't budge."

The chill spread quickly up Roxie's left arm and then shivered through her entire body. "It's freezing."

"You're freezing. To the parlor, quickly." Meredith helped her stand and ushered her into the parlor. Max and Paulette hovered behind the two women until Roxie dropped onto the love seat.

Her veins turned to ice, reminding her of the icebergs she'd seen on a documentary ages ago. Creeping inexorably wherever they wanted to go, crushing and reforming into a solid block of ice. She couldn't control the shivering or the trembling. She wrapped her arms around herself to no avail. Her teeth clicked together as the cold intensified until she couldn't bear it. Couldn't speak from the uncontrollable movements of her body as a result.

"Paulette, grab the afghans from the sewing room." Meredith sat down beside Roxie and wrapped her arms around her, pulling her back against her own body heat. "Hold on, Roxie. We'll warm you up yet."

Paulette ran out of the room, her footsteps pounding down the hall.

Max wordlessly raced to the fireplace and added more wood, stoking the flames into a roaring fire in moments. Paulette clattered back into the room with several wool crocheted afghans and tucked them in around the two women on the sofa. Roxie tried to thank her cousins for helping her but failed. Their efforts would be in vain. She would freeze to death. Only Leo could save her. But he'd turned his back. Fled. Left her to suffer the feared consequences.

She opened her mouth to warn the others but a spasm of intense cold burned through her. Ripping pain through every cell and fiber. She tried to call out Leo's name but couldn't hear her own voice. Then all went black.

Chapter Ten

The Hideaway was hopping when Leo yanked open the door and marched inside. Who knew Friday nights in Roseville brought so many out to eat and drink in the depressingly cheerful restaurant? Anger and hurt tornadoed in his core. He went straight to the small bar at the back and slid onto one of the high stools.

The bartender, a young man with orange tipped spiky hair, sidled slowly closer. The nametag on his salmon polo shirt read Sam. He couldn't be more than a few years out of high school, with such a baby face. Did he even shave? Leo felt ancient by comparison even though they could have gone to school together. *Had* they gone to school together? He'd pushed memories of high school so far into the recesses of his brain he'd never know unless he asked. And he didn't give a damn about whether they had.

"What can I get you?" Sam drummed his fingers on the counter. "Looks like you've had a day."

"Whiskey, neat." Leo scowled at him, his brows heavy over his eyes. Was it so obvious how he felt?

Sam flipped over a rock glass and poured whiskey into it, sliding the drink down to a halt in front of Leo.

The drive from the plantation into town had given Leo time to stew over the terrifying thought of returning to the place of his stupid crime. What he'd said about living with the result of losing his powers every day was more than merely true. He longed to have his powers back, to be whole again. Now that Peggy Golden had died, the last hope for being forgiven and having his powers restored had died as well. To go back to where he'd fouled out on his future proved unthinkable.

He'd tried to ignore the harsh reality he'd discovered upon his return to Roseville. Pushed it aside, still trying to be the man he'd become in spite of everything. He had a successful career with the respect of his teammates, his own luxurious condo in Atlanta, and even a few friends to hang out with upon occasion. But he still felt less than himself without the abilities he'd been born with. His mental acuity and prowess had languished as a result of nonuse. Sure, he'd become physically strong and fast, but nothing compared to what his powers would do for his strength and speed. If he had his abilities back, he'd hone them and use them to be a better man, warlock, friend. Maybe even husband one day.

Almost worse than losing his powers was knowing he'd so deeply disappointed his father. His dad had been his staunchest ally throughout his childhood and teen years. Had supported his desire to leave and be a pitcher for the Braves. Until he'd learned of Leo's misstep, of using his ability to secure himself a position on the varsity team. Grief and sadness added lines to his father's face within days of being informed by Peggy Golden of Leo's terrible transgression. Even the Order of Witchery Lore had looked down their long noses at him after word spread. Seemed everyone turned against him for one small infraction.

He took a big sip of whiskey and held it in his mouth for a moment, savoring the bite and smoky flavor. Swallowed to let it burn down his throat, hopefully burn away the pain inside.

Better to leave Roseville and all the memories flooding through him. Get back to his real life and forget the past. When the question of "fight or flight" entered his mind, the answer was simple. Flight. He'd leave Roxie to finish the quest without him, despite what her mother's note claimed. She couldn't insist from the grave, after all.

Leaving Roxie to complete the task he'd committed to helping her with. Which meant he'd be disappointing her again as well. He'd done the same thing six years ago. He'd shrugged off the pain of her walking away from him after accepting his proposal of marriage. Tried to understand her need to remain in Roseville with her family instead of loving him enough to marry him, be with him forever despite his misstep. He took another gulp of whiskey to try to burn away the hurt and dismissal.

He thought back to the events after he came to in the Golden living room. He'd struggled to the couch, Roxie joining him to hug him and ask about his well-being. He'd pushed her away, still reeling from what he considered her betrayal. They argued, every word of anger and accusation piercing and hurtful. He recalled the dialogue with utter clarity but refused to replay the script in his mind. At the time, he'd meant each word and hoped each would inflict the kind of agony his body and mind endured. He'd ended the disagreement once and for all. Severed their engagement and told her he would leave the next day. Go away and never return. Two days before the senior prom. The rented tux hung in his closet and her wrist corsage waited in the fridge, but he didn't care. Couldn't stay where he wasn't wanted.

He sipped the potent drink and wiped his mouth with the back of his hand. A hand landed on his shoulder, drawing his attention from his misery to the friendly grin of

Mitch Sawyer. Tall, dark blond, and handsome, Mitch's nearly black eyes crinkled at the corners as he occupied the next stool.

"What are you doing sitting here all alone?" Mitch motioned to Sam who nodded in response.

"Debating." Everything about his life, his past and his future. Another gulp and then he motioned to Sam for a refill.

"What exactly?" Mitch pivoted on the stool so he could look at Leo without turning his head.

"The notion of fight or flight." Leo nodded a thanks to Sam as he replaced the empty glass with a fresh one and set Mitch's draft beer in front of him.

"What are you fighting?" Mitch hefted his frosted glass mug and peered at him, resting one elbow on the bar.

Leo sipped his whiskey, delaying his response while he considered how much to share. Would he listen without passing on what he heard to Beth? Or the others? Seeing the group of friends and family gathered together, laughing and sharing everything openly, worried him. If he stayed— which he couldn't see doing the way things were—he'd be much like the other men without magic or powers. He'd be just another guy, a normal male without anything special to his name. But living among other witches like he used to be.

Since he wasn't planning to stay, then why not share with the guy? Even if he told, Leo would be long gone. He took another sip and swallowed. Then he told Mitch everything he'd been mulling over for the past hour.

Mitch listened in silence, sipping his beer and nodding occasionally. When Leo finally stopped, Mitch gave him a rueful grin. "That's a lot to untangle. But you're smart. I know you'll make the right choice."

"I'm heading home tomorrow." Leo clenched the half-empty glass with both hands. "It's not worth staying and trying to fit my square into the round hole of this place."

"Whatever you do, you have to own your past. Moving away didn't make that past problem go away. You can't change it." Mitch drained his beer and signaled for another. "But you can move forward to a better future. However you define it."

"Seems like a moving target." He grabbed a handful of roasted peanuts from the small bowl on the bar, juggling them in his hand. "I don't think my aim is good enough."

"You might need a bit of instruction, and then some practice." Mitch tapped his bottle to Leo's glass. "But I believe you'll find a way."

"I'm not so sure."

Leo examined the rock glass as if inspecting it for flaws. Mitch's sudden appearance in the bar seemed timed to thwart his plan to escape. Or was it simple coincidence? He sipped his drink, aware of the groom at his elbow. The wedding weeks away. Mitch teetered on the verge of becoming a member of the family coven he always thought he'd be part of with Roxie as his wife. He'd harbored the expectation of spending his life with her for so long he couldn't imagine a future without her in it. Even though he'd made a life in another place, he now realized he'd always known he'd return. To her. Without her life held no meaning, no joy, no love.

"So which is it, fight or flight?" Mitch pinned him with a humorous, knowing look.

Part of him wanted to flee back to his condo and hide from the pain of his past. But Mitch had a point. Doing so wouldn't change the past, wouldn't remove the hurt. In fact, it surprised him to realize some of the pain had lessened during the time he'd spent with Roxie. Remembering the good times they'd shared. Creating happier memories together. He'd even been reminded of how he'd imagined what their life together might be like, settling down in her house or perhaps fixing up his father's for them to share.

Being with her until they were old and gray, sitting in the proverbial rocking chair on the front porch of home. He stared at Mitch, seeing clearly for the first time.

When had he chosen without being aware? He really had only one option.

"Running away isn't going to help so much as suppress the pain." Leo tapped a finger on his glass in a staccato rhythm. "You've helped me realize. I'm staying and working this out once and for all. Despite the fact I had no intention of doing so when I came in here angry as a hornet."

"Trust me, I understand. When I came to Roseville, I had no intention whatsoever of staying. But then I met Beth and everything changed."

Leo cast a sideways glance at the man beside him. "For the better?"

"Most of the time." Mitch cocked his head to one side for a second and grinned. "Wedding planning is far more complicated than it should be."

"So I've heard. The honeymoon?" He bumped the nearly empty rock glass on the bar as he chuckled. "To go or not to go, that is the question."

"She can be stubborn when she wants something badly. Like when she decided to be my partner at airplane repo. Man!"

"Roxie told me she went overboard a bit. But it all worked out, right? So, what is it you want?" Leo drained the glass and pushed it away. "To go or not to go?"

"I want to take her somewhere exotic, but she doesn't want to go." Mitch slowly shook his head and then downed the rest of his beer. "She's always wanted to travel and now she's become a homebody. I don't understand."

Leo detected mild uncertainty in the timber of Mitch's voice. With the number of phone calls Roxie had received from Beth over the last few days regarding disputes between the couple, perhaps the earlier disagreement was inevitable. How much would Mitch and Beth disagree and ultimately fight after they were married? Roxie believed they needed to learn to compromise and he had to agree. But compromise takes two willing parties.

"No explanation from her?"

"She only will say it's not the right time to travel." Mitch pulled his wallet from his front pocket and opened it. "Sometimes I wonder if we're doing the right thing."

"The right thing?" Leo frowned at him as he noted the regret underlying his statement. "What do you mean?"

Mitch checked to make sure no one could overhear their conversation, leaning closer before replying. "Marriage."

"Are you having second thoughts?" Peering at the very serious man gazing at him, Leo saw he considered calling off the wedding. "Does Beth know?"

"No, and don't say anything." Mitch grimaced and sadly shook his head. "We're just always bickering or can't agree. But I love her to death. I'd break her heart if I walked away but I can't help but worry about our future."

"If you love her so very much, you'll find a way to make it work. Find a way to discuss and come to an agreement you can both live with. If you can't, then you know it's not going to work in the long run. Better to cut and run than be miserable for the rest of your life."

"Yeah, you're right." Mitch frowned into the bottom of his empty glass.

"You know it." Leo motioned to Sam for his tab. "I suppose I should head back to Twin Oaks."

"Back to solving riddles?" Mitch set his glass down. He fished his wallet out of his pocket to lay several bills on the bar.

"That and one other place." He'd have to face what he hated most but with Roxie at his side, he knew without any doubt he could do anything. Would face any threat or trial.

Including the damn quest spell. He retrieved his wallet from his back pocket and pulled out enough to cover the tab and tip for Sam. "The one place on earth I never wanted to go."

"Where is that?"

Leo met Mitch's quizzical expression with a wry smile. "High school."

He closed the front door at Twin Oaks and paused in the large foyer as he tried to decipher the frantic voices floating from the double parlor to greet him. He detected alarm in the tone. Striding quickly to the room, he hesitated in the open doorway. Meredith embraced a blanket-wrapped Roxie on the love seat, while Paulette hovered uselessly nearby. A blazing fire heated the room to sauna conditions. Max glanced up and frowned at Leo.

"About time." Max crossed the room to glare at him. "Where have you been?"

"I needed to think." He resisted folding his arms in a defensive move against the antagonism evident on the other man's features. "What happened?"

"We don't know."

"Leo, finally." Paulette motioned to him to approach her. "Roxie passed out and she's so cold."

He hurried to stand beside Paulette, peering down at the far too still form in Meredith's tender clasp. "How long has she been like this?"

"Since you left." Meredith aimed troubled eyes at him, tears glinting in the firelight. "The bracelet glowed and then turned cold. She's barely breathing and her pulse is faltering."

"We tried to remove the bracelet but it won't come off." Paulette shrugged helplessly. "What do we do?"

"How should I know?" Leo had no experience with frozen women. A cold shoulder, sure. Even a frosty look.

But Roxie's condition defied reason. He had no way to break the enchantment attached to the bit of jewelry. No powers at all. A chilling thought flashed through his befuddled mind. "The bracelet, you said?"

"Yes." Meredith regarded him with hope in her expression. "Why?"

Consequences. His heart fell to his feet as regret and fear swamped his core. "It's my fault."

He'd left Roxie alone and her mother's spell punished her for his betrayal. Roxie had warned him repeatedly about the spell's requirement of teamwork. Of staying together until they'd completed the treasure hunt. He'd stayed in the general vicinity of town, but not at her side. Something had changed since the last time they'd spent time apart. He skimmed through what had transpired between them and suddenly realized it was the bracelet. Only after she'd put it on had the more stringent requirement of staying in close proximity to each other become invoked. So when he'd stormed out in a huff and drove miles away, Roxie had been punished. For what he'd done. His stomach lurched at the guilt flooding through him.

Meredith shifted to rub her hands on Roxie's arms under the pile of afghans. "Because you walked out on her?"

He nodded slowly seeing the chastisement in her set jaw. "Any ideas how to fix this?"

Max joined him with a frown drawing down his brows. "Kiss her? It worked for Sleeping Beauty."

"Fairy tales? That's the best you've got?" Paulette spun to glare at the two men. "She could die if we don't do something. Soon."

"As cliché as it might sound, it can't hurt to try." Leo blew out a breath as he looked at each of the others. The deep connection he once shared with her might prove her salvation. If it still existed. "Right?"

"Go ahead then." Paulette flung a hand out in dramatic invitation to kiss the unconscious woman. "Thaw the lady with thine hot lips."

Ignoring the sarcasm, Leo swallowed as he moved closer. Leaned over the pair of women. Caught the intent expression on Meredith's face as he inhaled and then pressed his lips to Roxie's cold ones. Held still to warm her lips for a long moment. Finally pulling away enough to inspect her reaction. Nothing. She didn't move. Didn't flash open her eyes to scold him or love him. He ended the failed endeavor with a sigh as he straightened, feeling foolish and scared.

"Worth a try." Max shook his head. "Now what?"

Leo stared down at the woman he'd loved all of his life. Took one of her hands in his, holding on. Refusing to let go. To give up. All of the life they'd shared and the years they hadn't. He'd loved her with his entire being. Even when he denied his feelings. Even when he'd been angry and hurt. He'd never stopped loving her. She couldn't die.

Leo caught Max's worried look and slowly shook his head. "No clue."

"Wait…" Meredith cast a desperate yet hopeful glance at Leo. "She's not as cold now."

A seedling of hope poked its head from the depths of Leo's soul. He sought Roxie's face for any sign of movement, of an eyelash flickering, a change to her passive expression. Any hint of life remaining, or reborn. He squeezed her fingers, willing her to awaken.

"Roxie. Roxie!" He leaned closer, kissed her cheeks, her forehead. "Come back to me."

Saw the glimmering of pink washing over her cheeks. Meredith rubbed his woman's arms more energetically as Roxie moaned faintly. So softly it might be his imagination creating the sweet sound.

He closed his eyes, hoping for a miracle. Her voice always soothed him when troubled. The melodic cadence of her speech entranced him like no other person in all the world. He'd witnessed the maturing of the sound of her voice from her little girl voice, so high and clear, to the dulcet sound of her current tone. Had he imagined her awakening, of calling his name?

"Easy now. I've got you." Meredith's voice pulled him out of his musings.

Hope surged when he saw Roxie's eyes move side to side under her closed lids. Her lashes fluttered briefly as she stirred in Meredith's gentle embrace. Then her eyes opened and met his gaze, blinking slowly.

"Roxie." He knelt beside the love seat to lay his hands on top of the blankets. "Roxie."

What else could he say? He'd failed yet again to do the right thing. To be the man she needed. To ask forgiveness seemed too little. Too selfish. He buried his face in the soft fabric and sobbed. She shifted beneath him but he was too ashamed to raise his head, look into her eyes. Then a hand rested on his hair and he stilled.

"Leo..." Roxie's voice, like a Siren luring wayfarers, raised his eyes to meet her steady gaze. "You came back."

He stared into those beautiful soft hazel eyes. "I'm staying, too."

Meredith gasped. "Oh my, not again." She indicated with her head Roxie's left wrist.

Leo aimed a disbelieving look at the bracelet which softly glowed for several seconds and then faded to normal gold. "What just happened?"

"You came back." Roxie gave him a wry grin as she tiredly pushed at the afghans. "Ending the punishment for not being together."

"I'm staying with you." Leo helped lift the three thick blankets off of his woman, tossing them onto one of the side chairs. "We need to finish this quest."

She sat up straight and shifted away from Meredith's side. She regarded him silently and then nodded once. "Yes, we do."

He gulped back the rising gorge at the next admission. But he had to ensure she never faced such dire consequences ever again. Not because of anything he'd done. He'd do absolutely anything to keep her safe. So he looked her in the eye and smiled. "Tomorrow we go back to school."

Chapter Eleven

$\mathcal{A}$ strange silence blanketed the sleeping baseball field the next morning. More than the gently falling rain dampened the expanse of green grass and baseline. Leo helped Roxie step out of the car, keeping her hand in his after she stood beside him. Rain beaded on her dark blue jacket and her loose hair. The warmth of her fingers in his hand swelled his heart with happiness.

"It's so quiet." Roxie perused the ball field. "Should we be here?"

Denuded of the bases, the infield seemed stark and vulnerable. No white baselines waited to judge whether the hit went fair or foul. The dirt track hugging the infield lay pocked and puddled, not raked smooth ready for runners to try to make it to home base. A flock of birds darted and swirled across the gloomy sky, the only sound and movement. He had the impression of being backstage watching the actors prepare for their roles, being someplace he didn't actually belong.

"It's off season. Who'll know?"

"I have the oddest feeling." Roxie squeezed his hand. "Like it's waiting for us."

"Let's get this over with." He looked around, debating on where the next charm might be hidden. "Where do we start?"

"Let me try my sensing, see if I can narrow the options anyway." She closed her eyes and spread her hands wide, palms catching the light rain.

Leo shifted his weight to one hip, tapping his forefinger silently on his crossed arms, while Roxie reached out with her senses. Searched with her mind for remnants of magic, traces of the original spell her mother may have used. If only he had his powers back, he could help her. Together their combined powers might pick up some tiny residue. Slowly she lowered her arms and opened her eyes.

"Well?" He dropped his arms to snare her hand in his again.

"Sorry. Nothing yet again." She shrugged as she clasped his hand tighter for a moment. "We'll have to do it the hard way."

"I wonder if she hid it on the field somewhere." He glanced toward the beckoning diamond. The place he could relax and be at home. Until his transgression tainted the experience for him forever. Stirred dread in his heart at the thought of reliving the painful memories. "That's where I'd think she'd hide it, anyway."

If he could go back in time, would he change his actions knowing the ramifications? Definitely. He longed to play ball knowing he'd achieved his goals without the cloud of perceived magical assistance. The resulting insecurity regarding his talent haunted his actions, pushed him to excel to prove himself worthy of the praise he'd received.

"One problem. The gate to the field is locked."

"Let's try somewhere else first, then." He smirked at her. "No sense tempting fate by trespassing if we don't have to."

"Don't even think about it." Roxie shook her finger at him. "We're not breaking in."

"Unless we have to." He squeezed her fingers to let her know he was joking. Sort of. "Where do you suggest we look?"

She stared at him for several seconds before lifting her chin. Choosing to refrain from further chiding. "Mom knew how I devoured snow cones from the concession stand while you played." She pulled the hood up on her raincoat as the rain fell harder. "Let's try looking around there."

He doubted they'd find anything but better to humor her than act on his growing suspicion as to the charm's location. Besides, the delay gave him more time with her, holding hands. He led the way to the shuttered building. Imagined the delicious aromas of fries and burgers grilling. His mouth watered at the memory of slaw dogs and fresh lemonade. "Best dogs ever."

The concession side of the two-story red block house stood empty, its heavy metal awnings closed and secured. The other side of the building provided a backstop for several sets of metal bleachers. Hunkered fifty feet behind the right field dugout, the sturdy building doubled as a storm shelter in case of tornadoes. A warm embrace from a strong, loving father in scary times. How often had he stood beneath those metal sheets waiting for a sizzling hot dog with cole slaw piled on top? Windows on the upper floor glinted in the rainy sunshine. An intriguing phenomenon which never failed to amaze him. Sunshine and rain simultaneously, like Mother Nature laughing and crying at the same time.

"I don't even see a nook let alone a cubby hole." Roxie scanned the front of the building methodically as she held her hood in place.

"It could be camouflaged like the one at the theater." He slid his gaze across the building. "Hidden in plain sight."

Nothing. No chinks in the old man's armor where a small box could be hidden. His lightweight jacket didn't hold the rain at bay, his shoulders chilling as water seeped through. He shivered. "This is stupid."

She looked sharply at him. "What is?"

"We should just go to the field like I said." He pivoted to face the direction of the distant gate. "That's got to be where she'd put it."

"You think one of the dugouts?"

"Home team." He bobbed his head several times and then started walking, pulling her along with him. "Come on. We're going in."

He strode quickly, knowing success waited in the home team dugout somewhere. Where else would conjure the most repentance possible? Needle him for the error of his ways. Remind him of all he'd lost as a result of his transgression. Surely Peggy Golden would force him to return to the exact location of his crime against witchcraft. They must explore the dugout.

When they reached the gate, he dropped her hand and lithely vaulted over to land heavily on the other side. He grinned at her with a wave of his hand at the rattling gate. "Your turn."

She gawped at him for a moment. Then shook her head. "I won't climb over a gate."

"Or can't?" He propped his fists on his hips. "I thought you could do anything."

"It's illegal."

"We're not going to vandalize the place. Just look around." His grin disappeared the longer he stared at her. Why didn't she understand? "We have to."

"We should find a janitor, see if he'll let us in for a minute." She crossed her arms and studied him with a stubborn expression.

"And what reason would you give him?"

She opened her mouth to reply and hesitated, then snapped it shut.

"Exactly." Leo moved to grip the top of the metal gate. He plastered his best pleading puppy look on his face. "Come on. Please?"

"I'm not as athletic as you." She swallowed hard as she sized up the height of the horizontal metal bars. "I don't think I can make it over without hurting myself."

"Use your magic to help you." Somehow he had to convince her to try. "It's okay."

"No, it's not." She grabbed hold of the top of the gate, and shook it. "I don't..."

"Hey, you! Stop right there."

The bellow shot panic through Leo as he raised his eyes to spot a man running toward Roxie. She spun around in time to attempt a smile at the angry gray-haired man. Leo clambered back over the gate to stand by her side. No way would he let her take the heat for his actions.

He peered closer at the tall guy with his close-cut hair, trim goatee, and icy blue eyes. A tremor wiggled through him. Coach Bart Griffin. The same man who'd selected Leo based on magic, gave a young man hope for a stellar career based on smoke and mirrors, not talent.

"Coach." He regarded his former instructor with a tentative smile. "It's Leo King."

Shock registered in the widening of Coach's eyes and the open mouth. But he quickly recovered. "Leo King? You're all grown up." He extended his hand to Leo, who accepted the greeting in kind. "What brings you back here?"

He couldn't provide an honest answer to his coach's question but he could make up another reason just as valid in his mind. The rain fell harder, deepening the chill. Or was it the memory of tricking the coach into giving him a chance? He swallowed hard and tilted his head toward Roxie. "You remember Roxie Golden? I'm visiting and wanted to relive some fond memories."

"Hey, Miss Golden." Coach nodded at Roxie and then addressed Leo again, his brows lowering. "By jumping the fence?"

Leo shrugged, striving for nonchalance in the face of the authority before him. "Can you blame me for wanting to be back on the field?"

Coach studied him like a tear in the seam of a baseball, ready to throw it away rather than attempt to fix the fraying threads. "Really? I thought you played for the Braves now. Why would you want to come back here?"

"Well—" Why indeed?

"Excuse me." Roxie sidled closer to Leo, aiming a bright smile at the coach. "But I can explain."

Leo arched one brow at her and then motioned for her to continue. Her clever mind must have spun a new thread in the precarious web of deceit. The quirk of her brow hinted at an underlying subtle method she planned to employ to reassure the man. This ought to be good.

Tugging her hood closer around her face to keep the rain off her cheeks, Roxie prayed for inspiration. What possessed her to claim to have a valid reason for them to go onto the field in off season? In the rain, no less. Striving for confidence, she pushed her shoulders back and smiled at the coach. Reached out to him with her mind to gauge his reaction to what she was about to say.

"See, this is where Leo kissed me the first time." She slanted a glance at Leo and then met the older man's gleaming eyes, felt his curiosity mingle with wariness. "Now that he's home, he wanted to show me how much he wants to rekindle our relationship."

Coach Griffin studied her, searching her expression. He slowly shook his head, arms folding over his strong chest. "I don't believe you, my dear. Now you two should run along. Find someplace else to smooch."

A flash of light behind the coach drew her eye to where a school employee trundled a wheelbarrow toward the huge dumpster beside the block building. Pausing in the steady rain to wipe a rag over his uncovered, short-cropped hair, the young man met her curious gaze. She looked closer and quickly skimmed his entire person, spotting the tell-tale ring on his pinky as he lowered his hand from drying his head to briefly press the center of his chest in the OWL salute. His gray eyes fairly glowed in the gloomy light of the rainy day. Silently indicating he approved of the direction she'd taken he turned away and then disappeared before her eyes. She blinked in astonishment but then gathered her wits about her. Intentions confirmed, Roxie dragged her attention back to the coach.

"Wait, sir!" Roxie stepped closer, one hand raised to prevent him from walking away. Or calling security. "There's one more thing."

She didn't dare look at Leo. Kept her attention on the distrusting coach as she summoned her powers to persuade into play. Nothing too much, a mere nudge toward agreeing with her so they could finish what her mother had started. Bart Griffin watched her warily. She broadened her smile and lowered her hand as she reached into his mind with a fleeting touch, urging compliance. Sensed when his resistance weakened and then continued with her plea.

"The other reason we're here is because my deceased mother left a note of some kind in the dugout. I found a mention of it the other day among some papers. Please, I need to know what message she's left me from beyond the grave."

While not the whole truth, her mother had led them to the baseball field and the dugout. Had left them a charm and a note, waiting for them to locate both. The specific details the older man need not know. He would throw them out if she told him the complete truth. Maybe even call the police because he thought them crazy.

"When would she have done so?" The frown on the coach's face lightened with curiosity.

"I'm not sure." Roxie hesitated to tell him how long ago it might have been because he'd be less likely to believe her. But his hand slid into the case on his hip, fingering the cell phone hidden inside. Pulse pounding, she kept her composure intact by concentrating on the truth underlying her statements. "Sometime before she died is all I know."

Coach lifted the flap on the phone case, then let it snap closed. Instead of his phone, he pulled out a key ring and, muttering to himself, indicated for them to follow him. He unlocked the gate and pushed it open. "You've got two minutes."

Relief swept through Roxie. "Thanks so much. Come on, Leo."

She led the way through the jangling gate and toward the home team dugout. Leo jogged beside her as they dashed for the few steps leading down behind metal bars separating the higher field from the sunken pit.

"No kissing, either!" Coach Griffin hollered after them, followed by a deep chuckle.

Roxie huffed a laugh to herself. The old fart was a softy whether he admitted it or not. She skimmed her gaze around the interior of the dugout, past the long benches lining the rear wall. Over the junction box for the electrical connections. Finally lighting on the rows of wooden cubbies hung on the rear wall for the players to stash gloves, hats, and whatever other small items when not needed.

She waved toward the cubbies, then grabbed hold of Leo's hand. "One of those probably."

She inserted their joined hands into each square, one after another as seconds ticked by loudly in her mind. She encountered gum wrappers, a nearly empty can of face black, and several spider webs. No box. No note. No charm.

"One more minute, you two." The gruff voice bellowed again, warning ringing in each syllable.

"Where the hell is it?" Leo squeezed her hand.

She scanned the dugout again and then gasped. "There."

Dragging him behind her, she hurried to one end where a phone hung inside a black metal box. She stumbled over the two shallow steps up from the team benches to the coach's stool. Leo steadied her until she regained her balance. Grabbing his arm, she paused long enough to calm her agitation then dashed the last few strides to the phone box.

Without a word, she shoved their joined hands inside to search around the phone. The communication between Leo and Coach hadn't happened on the phone, but when the coach chose him, the news had been relayed by phone to the office. Surely the charm box hid somewhere around the device used to propagate the crime.

"Fifteen seconds and then I'm coming in."

Frantic, Roxie poked around in every corner, running their fingers along the outside of the phone itself. Searched underneath. Above. On the outside of the box. Top. Right side. Bottom. She froze and then snatched hold of the cool object attached to the bottom of the metal box.

"Got it." She held the box on the palm of her hand and gloried in the find. A silver oval box with daisies inscribed on the lid. Dying to open it, she sighed and shoved it inside the bag on her hip. "Let's get out of here."

Leo smiled at her, eagerness in his shining eyes. "Before he drags us out."

They trotted up the stairs to the infield and on to where the coach halted inside the fence.

"About time. Now scoot." Bart Griffin ushered them back out to the sidewalk, locking the gate behind him. "And Leo?"

"Yes, Coach?" He paused to pivot toward the older man's serious expression.

"Don't ever jump onto my field again. Understood?"

"I promise, Coach Griffin." Roxie intervened with a wave and a smile. "I won't let him."

"See that you keep him in line, miss." The coach lifted one brow slowly and then smiled. "Be happy together. You're a cute couple."

"Thank you, sir." Roxie turned back to Leo and saw him smiling gently. How had he interpreted the coach's demand? She didn't want to contemplate such matters standing out in the pouring rain. "I'm tired of being wet. Let's go."

Back in the car, she flipped her hood back. Leo started the car to let the heat remove the chill from their bodies. The windshield fogged from the moisture combined with the body heat, affording them privacy as she opened the box.

She lifted a feathered arrow charm from the velvety cushion, angling it one way and another to appreciate the fine detail of the jewelry. Her mother's taste proved impeccable, she could say that much about the individual charms.

"I'll attach it if you'll give it to me." Leo held out his palm and Roxie dropped the arrow on it. He shifted so he could reach the bracelet and soon had the fifth of six charms in place. The bracelet glowed with more light and warmth than before, slowly fading back to the normal luster of gold. "So where to now?"

"Let's see." She unfolded the small square of gold paper. She scanned the contents and then bit her lip before reading it out loud.

Words can harm and heal;
Power lies within their reality;
Care and constraint is paramount
When desires conflict unless
This is clear and open.
What am I?

"Well, that's clear as muddy water." Leo tapped the steering wheel and regarded her for several moments. "I've no clue what that means. So where do you want to go?"

"Take me home and we'll grab some lunch and try to figure this out." She studied the lines again as he drove out of the parking lot and turned toward Roseville. Her cell phone sang and she quickly answered. "Hey, Beth. We're head—Slow down. What's wrong?"

Leo shot a worried glance at her and then stared at the road.

Roxie sensed mounting grief and sadness from her sister. Confirmed by her next words.

"It's over." Beth sniffled and choked on her tears. "Can you come home? Please?"

"We're on our way." Roxie ended the call and pressed her lips together until they ached.

"What's wrong?" Leo sent her another concerned look.

"I'm not sure but it's bad. Hurry."

Chapter Twelve

S obs echoed from somewhere in the house and wrenched at Roxie's heart as she dropped her keys on the kitchen island. She yanked off her wet coat to hang on the coat tree by the door. "Beth? Where are you?"

Leo closed the kitchen door and hesitated by the island, meeting Roxie's quick glance with a serious expression. "Go find her. I'll make coffee."

"Perfect."

She pushed through the door into the hall, paused to listen, and then followed the sounds of anguish into the living room. So much hurt centered on the heart of the house. She hesitated in the open door, taking a minute to develop a clear sense of her sister's mental state. Beth lay on her stomach on the sofa, her face pressed into the crook of one arm, her chest heaving with each gasp and sob. Roxie sank onto a nearby chair and rested a hand on her sister's back.

"It'll be okay." She rubbed small circles between Beth's shoulder blades, slowly and gently. Like their mother used to do when they were little girls and had fallen and scraped a knee. Or when a boy ignored them. Or broke up with them. "I'm here."

The sobs continued for several minutes and then gradually became hiccups. Roxie kept up the soothing motion, patient for when the wave of sadness ebbed. Aware to her core of the distraught grief her sister grappled with each gasp. Minutes passed before Beth drew in a shuddering breath and pushed up to a sitting position. Eyes red and streaming, she sniffed as she leaned forward to hug Roxie.

"Want to tell me what's going on?" Roxie maintained a firm embrace on her strong yet emotionally fragile sister. "Why the waterworks?"

Snuffling, Beth gave Roxie one last squeeze and then sank against the sofa. "Mitch doesn't want to marry me."

Frowning at the surprise, Roxie peered at her. "What happened?"

Some of the sadness and hurt in Beth's face gave way for anger. "Your boyfriend. That's what."

"Boyfriend?"

"Leo. Don't be daft."

"Leo? What did he do?" The man had barely been out of her sight ever since he returned to Twin Oaks.

"He put doubts in Mitch's mind over a few drinks at the Hideaway." Beth sniffled, rubbing her nose with two fingers. "Told him it's better to end a relationship than be miserable."

"Why would Leo have told him that?" Roxie couldn't imagine Leo giving such advice.

Beth and Mitch hadn't appeared miserable in any way, except for maybe the disagreements on wedding plans. Nothing unusual about such matters when a couple started out on a new life, a new journey together. Nothing which couldn't be resolved.

Beth waved her hand as though brushing away an annoying pest. "Because I don't want to go on a honeymoon right now. I simply have the feeling it's not the right time. Something bad will happen if we do, and I don't want to risk it. Not until it feels right. But Mitch thinks I don't want to 'compromise,' Leo's helpful advice, and therefore we'll always be fighting."

"I've always trusted your psychic abilities. You've never failed to sense when trouble is brewing." Roxie blinked slowly at her stubborn sister. "But you have to admit he's right on one point. You do tend to stand your ground no matter what anyone else has to say."

An impish smile flashed onto Beth's mouth. "But I'm right. It's not the right time."

"Not the point and you know it." Roxie returned the smile and then stood, holding out a hand until Beth took it. "Come on. Leo's making coffee. Let's find out what his take on this is."

Strolling into the kitchen, the enticing aroma of fresh hot coffee filled her nostrils, making her inhale deeply with pleasure. Nothing smelled as good as hot coffee on a rainy afternoon.

"So, Leo, we have a question for you." Roxie strolled to the counter to pour coffee into mugs. She handed one to Beth and then followed her to sit at the red-clothed table. "Grab your cup and join us."

"I'm not guilty." Leo chuckled as he sank onto a chair and sipped from the steaming mug. "No matter what you might think."

Beth glared at him as she brushed imaginary crumbs across the table with the back of her fingers. "According to Mitch, you told him to end our engagement."

Leo shot back in his chair, eyes wide. "I did not."

"He's postponed the wedding in order to think about what you told him the other night." Beth leaned forward, searching Leo's shocked expression. "Do you deny you told him it was better to end a relationship than to be miserable?"

"That's not exactly what I said." Leo swallowed, his coffee forgotten, as he glanced between the two women. "I didn't tell him to end your relationship."

Roxie took a sip of coffee, letting the warmth seep through her core. "Then what did you say to make him postpone?"

"I didn't say anything. He was having his own doubts about the arguments you two have been having. I suggested that since you love each other so much you'd find a way to compromise."

"And if we didn't, then it would be better to stop the wedding." Beth pursed her lips and squinted at him. "How dare you meddle?"

"On the bright side," Roxie quickly said, "he postponed not canceled. We have time to change his mind back." She shot a look at Leo, suggesting with a raised brow his involvement in such an attempt. "Leo?"

He glanced confusedly at Roxie and then Beth and back again. "What do you want me to do?"

"He's the one who caused the problem in the first place." Beth aimed startled eyes at Roxie. "He can't fix this."

"I think he should be the one who talks to Mitch. Maybe ask Grant to go with you since he married into this sisterhood as well." The idea sprung from out of the blue but seemed a good one. "He may have some advice for Mitch that Leo doesn't. And there's strength in numbers."

"I doubt anything will work." Beth propped her chin on her palms, elbows on the tabletop. "Mitch seemed shutdown when I tried to talk to him about it."

"Leo will take care of it. He's good at guiding people." Roxie cut him a sarcastic glance and then patted Beth's arm. Her sister needed a distraction, something to take her mind off of her future and Mitch. "In the meantime, we found a new riddle. Want to help solve it?"

Beth dragged in a deep, deep breath and blew it out through her nose. "Fine."

Roxie rolled her eyes at her sister's adolescent behavior, refraining from calling her on it. Instead, she pulled out the latest slip of gold paper and laid it flat on the table. "Here's what it says."

Words can harm and heal;
Power lies within their reality;
Care and constraint is paramount
When desires conflict unless
This is clear and open.
What am I?

After she read it out loud, Roxie looked at Beth. "I think the first two lines refer to spells. What do you think?"

"Words that heal and harm and contain power in what they create." Beth thought for a moment and then nodded. "Yes, I think you're right."

"What does care and constraint have to do with spells?" Leo asked.

"I don't think that refers to the spells but to the conflicting desires." Roxie aimed her puzzled eyes at Beth. "Like when you and Mitch want different things. That's when you need to care about the other's feelings and use constraint on how you react. Make sense?"

Leo nodded as he smiled at Beth. "Lessons abound from your mother's clues. She was quite an insightful witch."

Beth rolled her eyes at Leo, making him laugh out loud. "Touché."

"But what needed to be clear and open?" Leo shook his head slowly, narrowing his eyes as he contemplated possibilities.

"Eyes?" Beth shrugged. "To be able to see how your actions affect others?"

"Maybe." Roxie tapped a finger against her chin in a regular rhythm, much like a metronome maintaining the beat. "Or…"

"What?" Beth peered at her, eyes gleaming. "You know, don't you?"

Roxie bobbed her head. "I think it's 'communication.' And since it's pointing to spells and the need for powerful words, it can mean only one place to go for the final charm."

Leo leaned forward, his expression anxious. "Where might that be?"

"OWL." Her sister's eyes widened while Leo's clouded. She speared him with her gaze. "What's wrong?"

"Why must you throw this in my face at every turn?" He huffed and jumped to his feet, the chair crashing to the floor behind him. "I'm aware I'm not a warlock any longer. You don't need to rub my face in it."

Stunned, she could only stare at him for a moment. Ever since he'd arrived in Roseville, he'd presented himself as put upon, as being forced to do things he didn't want to. As if she had invited him to waltz into the store with the demanding quest. Like it was her idea they spend so much time together. He'd started the proverbial ball rolling, not her. Then anger bubbled to the surface. How dare he? "I'm not doing anything to you."

Yanking the chair upright, he spun it around, set it in place, and leaned on it. "You're dragging me back in time to places I've avoided for a very good reason."

"Do you want to finish this quest or not?" Roxie leaned back in her chair and folded her arms, shooting a hot look at the frustrating man. "Stop dragging your feet."

"Drag my feet? Who jumped the damn fence to hurry up this process?" He glowered as his emotions played across his face.

What she sensed was more fear and discomfort than anger. Much like when forced to return to the ball field against his will. Against his preferences. He'd gone despite his reservations and embarrassment. He'd go again but only after he'd spluttered and protested. Then he'd not lose face by giving in to the inevitable. He'd go even if it meant doing so with the air of an aggrieved victim. She lowered her arms to rest her elbows on the table, chin propped on her fists while she studied him.

"You nearly got us arrested with that stunt." She grinned at the image of him jumping right back over to stand at her side. Chivalry apparently hadn't died. "It all worked out, right? So will this."

"Hold your horses, sister mine." Beth bumped her fist on the table, gaining both their attention. "What about Mitch? You promised to talk to him. Don't go running off on your quest and forget there's a wedding in limbo."

Roxie startled at the reminder. "The OWL headquarters isn't open over the weekend anyway." Covering her mistake. She hadn't put her sister's pain first. She had forgotten all about the need to have a conversation with Mitch. Chagrined at her lapse, she lifted her chin from her hands then pressed her palms on her thighs. "It's a bit late today. Leo, why don't you arrange to meet him tomorrow?"

Leo released the chair and rubbed his hands together as if he were washing them. "That gives me time to think of what to say to the guy."

Roxie would work on figuring out how they'd gain access to the Order without raising suspicion as to their motives. They weren't expecting her to march up to the door and demand entry. The only times she'd been inside her mother had invited her and her sisters for a special ceremony of some kind. How would she explain the need to poke around the shelves of books in the library, the depths of the vast quantity of microfiche and microfilm, or even more worrisome, the sacred ceremony room, the Grand Hall? All with a man who detested the very idea of setting one foot on the property let alone within the revered building.

"We'll drive to the Order on Monday if all goes as planned." Roxie attempted a smirk at Leo and then Beth but feared she'd failed. "If they'll let us in."

He couldn't do it. Not alone. But who did he trust to help him? What guy did he know who had an easy manner and way with words? Leo perused the backyard of the Golden home from the comfort of the conversation pit, contemplating his options. After pacing the small yard for far too long, he'd collapsed into a cushioned chair to think. He'd have liked to go roaming the city streets, burn off the bubbling over energy tightening his core as he explored the shaded residential neighborhoods. But he didn't know what else might happen if he moved too far from Roxie. Until the quest ended and the bracelet completed, he'd stick to her side. He'd never risk her life again.

The gardens displayed a few bedraggled roses clinging to the thorny vines climbing the privacy fence. Tucked in front of fragrant boxwood and low-growing unruly juniper bushes, white and yellow chrysanthemums provided bursts of color. The shed seemed dowdy among the fading flowers and evergreen bushes. Fallen leaves rustled and swirled in agitated eddies as spurts of wind caressed his cheek. The sight of the garden gradually going to sleep for the winter brought him not one ounce of pleasure as he mulled over his options.

First consideration was how to keep Roxie nearby but not involve her in the men's conversation. He needed her near but not in the room with them. While her empathic nature could prove useful, he worried Mitch would take it as interference. But he had to keep her close. Best if he could see her, know she remained safe and not suffering from the separation. They'd experimented earlier and discovered the bracelet didn't react when he walked as far as the street, but if he turned and started walking down the sidewalk it flared. Roxie had yelled for him to come back and he did at a run. Thus his choice of sitting in the yard to ponder. He needed to think but not inside.

A sounding board. That's what he needed. And he knew just the person. He pulled out his phone and called Twin Oaks. Half an hour later, Max strolled into the backyard carrying a six pack of cold beer.

"I've brought reinforcements." Max hefted the carrier as he approached where Leo had risen to greet him. "How you doing?"

"I've been better." Leo accepted the offered bottle and twisted off the cap. "Thanks for coming."

"What's the fire alarm about?" Max crossed to the other chair and settled down. "You sounded rather worried on the phone."

Leo sat on the armrest of the opposite chair, resting the cold bottle on his thigh. "Mitch has postponed the wedding, maybe forever."

"I heard." Max swigged the brew with a quick lift and swallow. "What's that have to do with you?"

"Beth thinks it's my fault. So I have to fix it. Fix him by convincing him to change his mind." Leo chuckled dryly as he shook his head. "Where do I start?"

"Man. That's a tall order." Max tapped the bottom of the bottle lightly on the armrest. "Do you know why he called it off?"

Leo shrugged, forcing his shoulders back down to their normal position. "I think so but there could be more to it than what he hinted at the other night."

Max's ears perked up and he stilled the tapping. "What other night?"

"He came in the Hideaway while I was there last Friday. You know, when Roxie had her attack."

He'd never forget that particular night as long as he lived. How upset and righteous he'd felt walking away.

How frustrated, hurt, angry. Then his remorse and chagrin upon learning what his selfish actions had caused in his absence. His lovely woman nearly frozen to death by his determination to wrest control from the enchantment and the spell.

"Go on." Max regarded him with the direct assessing gaze of a high-powered lawyer. "I'm listening."

"We were talking and he mentioned the bickering and never agreeing." Leo sucked in a fortifying breath and then blew it out. "I told him they'd either find a way to compromise if they love each other enough or it would be better to end it rather than live in misery."

Max didn't say a word. Merely stared at him as he swigged another gulp of beer.

"I know." Leo dragged his fingers through his hair and shifted to sit on the seat of the chair. "I screwed up big time."

"The only thing you can do is talk to him and apologize for putting wrong ideas into his head." Max's eyes glinted in the afternoon sunlight as he steadily regarded Leo.

"Will you come with me? Back me up?"

"I may have a better idea." Max leaned over to set his empty bottle on the patio.

"What's that?"

"Let's make it a party. Invite all the current and future brothers-in-law." Max angled his head briefly as he shrugged, his expression turning mischievous. "Make it seem more general than confrontational."

"Even though he's postponed the big day?" Leo patted his knee with one hand. "Don't you think he'll be suspicious?"

"I'm sure he will be but he'll come anyway. He likes us all." Max smirked at Leo. "He's a tough one. He'll think he can handle whatever we throw at him. He's probably right, too."

"Then what's the point if he comes already primed to resist whatever we say?"

"That's where we come in. No matter his reasons or objections, we've all been in love with one of the pack of five women we call family." Max touched a forefinger to his temple. "We know how to ease any concerns he may have. Leave it to us."

If it meant Leo didn't have to figure out what to say to counter his ill-considered advice, then great. "Go for it."

Max pulled out his phone and shot Leo a grin. "I'll send a group text to issue the invitation. Tomorrow at noon at the Hideaway?"

Leo nodded, pondering yet again how he'd keep Roxie near but not inside with them. But if Max could finagle the group lunch then he could manage something. But what?

With Leo busy outside with Max, the girls had gathered for a night in together. Roxie thought everyone could use the opportunity to discuss everything happening over the last week. A spur of the moment whim to be sure. Tara listed the choices for which Halloween movie they should put on. Beth debated whether to order pizza or put together finger foods. Meredith and Paulette arrived with wine, chocolate fondue and fresh strawberries to dip. Roxie puttered around the living room, rearranging furniture so everyone could reach whatever food ended up on the coffee table and they could all see the TV screen. And hoped Leo wouldn't spoil everything by coming in too soon.

Distraction. The best cure for indecision and anxiety. She plastered a grin on her face and scurried into the kitchen. Beth hung up the phone with a dusting of her hands as Paulette plugged in the small crockpot of chocolate to keep warm until after their early dinner. Tara mixed margaritas and handed them round in frosted glasses.

"We ready?" Roxie motioned to the group of chattering females and held the door open.

"Pizza on its way in fifteen." Beth sashayed through the door, heading for the living room with a stemmed glass held aloft. "Let's go, ladies!"

"Right behind you." Tara followed, trailed by the others. "Roxie, come on."

"Sheesh." Roxie let the door swing shut as she traipsed after her sisters and cousins into the living room. "This was my idea, you know."

"Slow poke." Beth chuckled at her as she nabbed an oversize pillow and tossed it in front of the couch. "We need some serious fun."

"What's the flick, Tara?" Meredith folded her long legs on the sofa, drink in hand. "Nothing too sappy, I hope."

"Hocus Pocus." Tara waggled the DVD case in her manicured fingers. "One of my must-see movies every fall."

"Rox, is Leo joining us?" The hesitant question drifted across the suddenly quiet room.

All eyes turned to Roxie. She swallowed and shook her head. "Not if I can help it."

The chatter resumed as Tara placed the disc into the player. The tension eased with each passing second. If he slipped into the house while the party continued, she'd give him some pizza and send him upstairs. Close by but not intruding. Although having him sleeping in her house, in the next room, could be considered intruding by default.

As the movie rolled on and the drinks were refreshed, the volume in the room—created by the laughter over the antics of the actors in the movie coupled with the friendly joshing between the women—increased to the point Roxie almost missed the doorbell. She scurried to the kitchen door to sign for the three large pizzas her sister had ordered. Was she expecting more company? They'd be eating pizza for a month.

She carried the boxes into the living room and set them on the low table in the center of the commotion. Then went back to the kitchen for paper plates and napkins. She had no desire to be washing dishes at the end of the evening. Grabbing a slice of veggie, she settled into a chair to eat and watch. Relaxed into the moment, letting the movie work its magic on her jangled nerves. Sitting at the back of the group, she could see how much the women in her life loved and cared for each other. After several minutes, she rested her head back and closed her eyes. Let her thoughts flow and her inner senses seek out underlying information not available to the normal five senses.

Then she detected an unusual tug on her probing sense. A deep concern. Worry. Question. She opened her eyes to see Beth studying her. Blinked awake and sat up.

"Tara, can you pause for a minute?" Beth waved a hand at her sister until the image on the screen stilled. "Thanks. I have a question for Roxie. I have to know."

"Now? Can't it wait? They're about to make the moon…" Meredith grumbled and then fell silent.

"What is it, Beth?" Roxie forced her hands to remain loose on her thighs despite the tension inside.

Beth bit her lip for a couple of seconds. "Does Leo blame you for breaking off the engagement? Is that why he's so dead set against working with you?"

"He's working with me. What do you mean?" Roxie frowned at her sister.

She shrugged in response. "I don't know. He seems…reluctant and yet obligated. What actually happened between you two? You never really talked about it."

"You were a kid, Beth. You didn't care then."

"I care now. Tell me." Beth wiggled around to face Roxie squarely. "I'm listening."

"The others probably don't want to hear this. Start the movie." She didn't want to talk about it. Ancient history.

Paulette leaned forward, her half-empty glass dangling in one hand. "I think we do want to hear this. Go on, Roxie. Tell us what happened between the two of you."

"You know most of it."

Meredith gave her an encouraging smile. "Tell us the rest."

Roxie made a face at the thought of dredging up the argument which ended their relationship. "The short answer is he broke the rules and I couldn't let him get away with using magic for his own benefit. I wouldn't have been able to trust him to do the right thing. Our parents agreed and decreed the results."

"Did you fight or did he simply walk away?" Tara clutched the remote like a knife, ready to use to defend herself.

"We fought. Said things we couldn't take back." Roxie heaved a sigh. "I wish I could. He ended our engagement two days before the prom."

Paulette gasped and set her glass on the table. "Did you go without him?"

Roxie closed her eyes for a moment and then opened them to stare at Paulette. "I went stag but I didn't dance. My heart had left with him."

She'd been asked many times. Pity dances. Or so she'd feared. Even Hans had tried to tempt her onto the dance floor but she'd stayed firm. Attending the senior prom had been a lifetime dream and she wouldn't let even Leo's actions stop her from realizing it. But she wouldn't be a laughingstock. Nor would she sit at home and cry over his desertion. He'd called her a traitor for betraying him to their parents. She'd had only his best interests in mind when she'd confessed his crime to her mother. As difficult as it had proven to be, she'd done it to help him correct his mistake. The price she'd paid for her role had been high. Losing him. She'd do it all again if the situation presented itself.

He needed to face the facts about the right way to use his abilities. She'd hoped their marriage would be forever. If it had happened. When he'd stormed away and word arrived he'd packed up and left town for the big city, she thought her heart would shatter into tiny shards. Somehow she'd managed to keep breathing, keep going to school and then to work. Until he'd come back and tossed her equilibrium into the abyss.

She speared Beth with a steady look. "Does that answer your question?"

Beth nodded slowly and then rose to cross the room. Pulled Roxie to her feet, and gave her a long sisterly hug. Tara soon joined them, wrapping her arms around their embrace. Meredith stood and deposited her glass on the table before adding her arms to the group hug. Then Paulette completed the group. They stood together for several moments, silent and supportive.

The kitchen door opened and slapped shut, footsteps nearing. With a collective sigh, the women dropped their arms and turned back to their seats. By the time Leo paused at the doorway to the living room, the movie was back on and they were chewing on pizza.

Roxie glanced up at him with a raised brow, hoping he'd move on. He winked at her and then continued up the stairs to his room. She snatched up her drink and took a long sip. Tomorrow would be soon enough to answer any more questions.

Chapter Thirteen

A nasal horn honked as Leo closed the door to his car parked in front of the Hideaway. The rust-bucket of a pickup rattled and coughed as it sped past him on its way out of town. Idiot. Shaking his head, he circled around to the passenger side and leaned down to chat with Roxie through the open window. A cool breeze flowed through the shedding trees spaced along the sidewalk, dried colorful leaves clustering in the gutter and up against the buildings.

"Thanks for understanding. I'll bring out your lunch in a few minutes." He kissed her upturned mouth and then pulled back.

"I wouldn't intrude on your guy talk. And I don't want to relive what this bracelet can do. So…" She slowly arched one brow at him. "I'm content as long as you promise to fix this."

He gripped the window frame. "We're going to. I promise."

Somehow. He still wasn't certain how Max intended to broach the topic let alone change Mitch's mind. He'd practiced a slew of arguments against the advice he'd given the unwilling groom. If only Leo still possessed his mind-reading ability he'd know how to persuade Mitch using his own arguments against him. Back in his teens, he'd have taken the even shorter route. A simple idea implanted in each of the couple's thoughts would encourage them to work together, find the solutions to their disagreements rather than split up. He'd learned better over the ensuing years. Forced suggestion would be a one-time thing and not lasting for the duration of their married lives. Not a good fix in the long term. No, they needed to come to the realization themselves and then put in the work.

"There's Zac and Grant. Hey guys." Roxie waved at the brothers as they strode up the sidewalk. Leo straightened to greet them with a handshake for each.

"You don't want to come in?" Zac regarded her with confusion in his expression.

"Not this time, thanks." Roxie grinned and settled more comfortably in her seat. "I'll be fine. You go on. Have a good lunch."

As the three men headed to the door, Max and Mitch hurried to join them. Within minutes they were all seated at a large table by the front plate-glass window, studying the menus as they waited for their drinks to be delivered by the gangly teenaged waiter. After placing their orders, including a sandwich and drink for Roxie, Zac cleared his throat.

"Leo, why did you make Roxie sit outside?" Zac's gaze remained steady as he regarded Leo. "It's not right."

"It's the best compromise we could come up with. She didn't want to join us but you know we can't be too far apart, either." He cast a glance at each of the men seated at the round table. "Not after what happened the other night."

"Right." Zac shot a look at Max, brows knit. "Why are we here again? Not that I mind having lunch with you all, just wondering why the urgency."

The waiter hurried up to the table with a large tray. He dealt out the drinks like a poker dealer and then marched away with the tray at his side.

"Why the urgency?" Mitch huffed a laugh as he picked up his steaming coffee. "I think I know."

"Spill." Grant fiddled with the silver knife, straightening it to align with the edge of the napkin it laid upon. "I'm curious, too."

"I imagine the girls wanted you to talk to me about not postponing the wedding." Mitch's eyes flashed as his gaze slid from one to the other, finally landing on Leo. "Right?"

"Yeah. I gave you some bad advice." Leo swallowed as he smiled ruefully at the wary man. Which of the many potential arguments should he bring to the table? "I was wrong to tell you to break it off if you couldn't work together. You love the woman and she loves you."

"You need to butt out, Leo." Mitch lifted his cup and pointed it at him. "You're not a part of this family."

Stung, Leo could only stare silently at the defensive and disgruntled guy. He was right. Mitch had been accepted into the fold. His place in the family was his for the taking. Leo had lost the chance to be part of the gregarious and growing family years ago. He scanned the faces at the table and then met Roxie's gaze through the window. Her light brown eyes carried a silent message, of hope and confidence in him. He nodded once as she smiled. Something inside him stirred, tugging on remembered magic and abilities, then quieted. Another odd twinge. He'd not experienced such a sensation until returning to Roseville. Connecting again with Roxie. Somehow he knew whatever was happening inside him had something to do with her. Longing to rush out to share with her his supposition, he squashed the idea as the conversation inside resumed. First things first.

"No call for such tones," Max interjected. "Leo is only doing what he must."

"To settle with Roxie." Mitch shook his head and then gulped his coffee, his expression guarded. He set his mug down with a thud. "It's not about what's best for Beth."

"You think postponing or, worse, canceling the wedding is in her best interests?" Grant cocked his head as he studied Mitch. "That's going to break her heart."

Mitch firmed his lips as he stared into the depths of his mug. "Better than fighting over every little thing."

Zak aimed his serious gray eyes at the bowed head of the tense man. "Mitch, it takes two to argue. Maybe you need to pick your battles more carefully."

Lifting his head slowly, Mitch regarded Zak for several seconds before his dark brown eyes softened ever so slightly yet retained their brittleness. "She makes everything into a crisis. It's tiresome."

"She's planning the biggest day of her life. Perfection is not good enough." Grant glanced at Zak and then Max. "Am I right?"

"Definitely. Mitch, you have to understand these women are something special. Even more so when they're working together." Max crossed his arms as he leaned back in his chair to contemplate the reluctant groom. "Beth loves you and has joined forces with her sisters to create a special day for you both."

"Seems like it's all about what she wants and not what I want." Mitch gulped down coffee and grimaced. He motioned to the passing waiter for a refill then shook his head. "Why won't she travel now when that's all she wanted to do only a few months ago?"

"The mysteries surrounding our lovely ladies are not to be understood by mere mortal men, Mitch." Leo chuckled at the surprise on the other man's face. "Trust me. As much as I would like to think I know Roxie after all of the years we've spent together, the truth is she continues to mystify."

The waiter returned bearing their meals on plates and a to-go box. He deftly handed them out, leaving the white Styrofoam carton and drink at Leo's elbow. After he left, Leo pushed back from the table and picked up the box.

"I'll be right back. Go on without me." Leo turned and strode through the restaurant and out the front door to pause beside his car. "You doing okay, Roxie?"

"I'm fine. Listening to music and playing a game on my phone. Oh, yum!" Roxie peered inside the box at the grilled ham and cheese sandwich then smiled up at him with a hint of mischief in her eyes. "Thanks."

"Looks like it might rain any minute." He dangled his keys into the window. "In case you want to put up the windows."

She took the keys and dropped them into the center console well. "Now scoot. You've got work to do."

He mock saluted with a grin of his own. "Aye, aye." He leaned in to kiss her quickly and then went back inside. Her easy-going nature soothed his ruffled conscience from making her sit outside. Even if it had been her idea.

"Each of them have unique talents," Grant said as Leo resumed his seat. "Beth has shown you how perceptive she is of potential events yet to come."

"So perhaps Beth is sensing a need to stay close to her sisters without even knowing the root cause." Biting into his Reuben, Zak chewed as his gaze drifted around the group.

Mitch's brows descended over his concerned eyes. "She is psychic."

"Exactly." Max pointed his half-eaten burger at Mitch. "We have learned to trust their instincts. Roxie has made a name for herself in the manipulation of phrases and spells. But none of the girls will leave her sisters on a whim."

A flash of light outside drew Leo's attention. He searched for the source but only saw Roxie sipping on her drink, her phone in hand. Perhaps she'd angled it and caught the afternoon sunlight just right to shoot a ray inside. She looked so lovely in the soft afternoon light, relaxed and enjoying the quiet Sunday afternoon in the small town. Her long brown hair glinting as she nodded to the beat of the music flowing around her. She turned to look at him, meet him with her brown eyes and a soft smile.

A flutter somewhere deep inside ignited a desire for the return of his abilities. A warm glow tickling the nerves and fibers of his being, awakening them to stretch and yawn as if from a long nap. Roxie winked at him and turned back to her game. Severing the tenuous connection and plummeting his hope down to despair at the realization he'd never have them again. Not without Peggy Golden to restore them.

Leo dragged his attention back to the conversation, puzzling over the sensations and sights of the last few minutes. Sure of only one thing: his feelings for Roxie had grown into a living thing in his heart. Purring and cuddling until he couldn't ignore any longer the depth of love he had for his woman.

"You know, you guys are right." Mitch sat back in his chair, resting his palms on either side of his sandwich plate. A slow half smile eased onto his lips. "I want to marry Beth. I've been an idiot. I'll call her and let her know the wedding is on."

"Really? What changed your mind?" Leo gaped at Mitch for a moment and then slapped his mouth shut. Events were transpiring quickly. Too quickly? "I mean, I'm glad for all concerned, of course, but why?"

Mitch waved his hands in an unconcerned manner. "I can't explain it but it feels right. You've all convinced me I overreacted."

"Good for you. I'm glad we could help." Max lifted his glass of cola in a toast. "To the happy couple."

The others lifted their drinks as well, Leo more slowly as his mind raced over the curious happenings of the past few minutes. Yet he didn't blame Mitch for his sudden change of heart. After all, Mitch did love Beth nearly as much as Leo loved Roxie. If Mitch could settle down and choose to spend the rest of his life in Roseville in order to be with Beth, perhaps Leo should reconsider his own plans.

"Congratulations again." Grant smiled as he tapped his glass against Mitch's mug. "I'm glad you'll be my brother before much longer."

"Hey, you already have a brother." Zak smirked at Grant and clinked glasses with him. "But I'm happy to have more brothers, too."

Max glanced at Leo with a brow lifted. "Will you be joining our brotherhood?"

The question gave him pause. He'd fought against the concept with all his might. Only he hadn't been strong enough to resist Roxie's allure. To resist his feelings for her no matter how much he denied them. He needn't bother cataloguing what aspects and features he loved. He loved everything about her. Loved her with all his heart and accepted her for who and what she was.

He glanced out to where she sat in the car and saw her gazing back at him, her expression unreadable.

Raindrops spotted the windshield, landing and blending together to create a blurry watercolor of the town square beyond. The sodden skies painted a gray backdrop to the shimmering red and yellow brick of the historic buildings surrounding the gray stone courthouse and the white gazebo which doubled as a bandstand in the summer. Few people scurried along the wet sidewalks on the quiet Sunday afternoon. Roxie snuggled into the creamy leather seat and tapped a finger in rhythm with the tunes in the sleek car. Glancing at the window where she'd been keeping tabs on the guys, she shifted to sit taller. Where'd they go?

Two taps on the window startled her into dropping her phone to bounce off her leg and down between the console and seat. She peered up at Leo's unsmiling features through the watery glass. He opened the door and leaned inside.

"Walk with me?" He held out a hand, waiting until she placed hers in his palm, and then clasped her fingers to help her ease out of the low-slung vehicle. "I kept my promise."

Standing on the brick paved sidewalk, Roxie handed him his keys and then clung to his hand as he pushed the car door shut. "The wedding is back on?"

He pocketed the keys and then maintained his gentle grasp of her hand as they strolled down the sidewalk toward the square. "Yes."

"Beth will be over the moon." She shot a quick glance at him, surprised by his terse reply. "Everything okay?"

"Of course."

He didn't act as if everything was fine. He seemed distant, preoccupied. In no hurry to reach his destination despite the light mist falling. She held her tongue, sensing he needed time to sort through whatever distracted him. She observed their surroundings, pleased by the townspeople's efforts to beautify the streets and sidewalks. Potted mums sat at each corner alongside the light poles. Pennants with town festival announcements hung listlessly in the rain from the poles. Several cars pulled up to the intersection, pausing to wait for the light to change. Other than the few vehicles, they seemed alone in town.

When they stopped at the corner to wait to cross the street, a figure emerged from beside the old theater. The long charcoal cloak concealed the person's gender as effectively as the raised hood hid their features. Moving wraith-like along the sidewalk, as if floating instead of striding, they slowly moved to stand beneath the awning of the drug store. Turning to face Roxie and Leo, the glint of gold flashed on one hand. Roxie stiffened at the sight, unsure if her instincts proved accurate or if she projected her fears upon the unidentified person.

"What's wrong?" Leo squeezed her hand and captured her gaze with his.

"Don't look but I think that person is watching us." She regarded him for a second, recognizing suppressed excitement in his expression. "Do you know them?"

"I doubt it, but let's not worry about it right now. I have something to tell you."

"But I have this feeling I should know them." She looked askance at the brooding figure and then back to Leo. "It's rather creepy and yet familiar all mixed together."

The crosswalk light changed and started counting down from fifteen seconds.

"Come on." Leo pulled her with him across the street and then up the few steps to the shelter of the gazebo. Once inside, he positioned her in front him, holding both her hands in his gentle grip. He studied her for several moments, his mouth gentling into a deprecating grin before sobering. He cleared his throat and the grip on her hands tightened.

"What is it?" Confused by his reluctance and silence, she searched his expression for some reassurance. "What's bothering you?"

He chuckled briefly and some of the tension in his eyes eased. "I'm not good at this, Roxie. I don't know where to begin. It's not something I'd planned when I woke up this morning."

A chill wriggled through her followed closely by a warmth in her core which spread to her necks and cheeks. Steeling her emotions, she waited for him to continue.

He shifted his grip on her hands to draw them to his chest, bringing their bodies within inches of each other. "I've tried to resist your allure, but I cannot deny any longer what I feel for you goes far deeper than it ever did when we were kids. I can't imagine living without you, Roxie. I love you and I need to be with you."

His grip on her hands tightened for a second and then relaxed as he leaned forward to kiss her lips with a slow, gentle pressure. The thrill swept through her as she angled her head back, inviting him to deepen the exploration of her mouth which he quickly accepted. The rainy world fell away as her eyelids lowered and all her senses tuned to the man holding her close. Slowly he eased away to gaze down at her, his eyes shimmering in the dusky light. She moistened her parted lips as she smiled.

"I love you, too, Leo." She'd waited so very long to be able to say as much to him again. Joy and relief whirled through her. Finally.

"Roxie…" He searched her eyes, his gaze dropping to land on each of her facial features before meeting her gaze again. "Will you marry me?"

A hush fell over the square. No traffic. No people. Except for the cloaked figure lingering across the square. Roxie shot a glance at the wraith and spotted the tell-tale indigo owl ring. She frowned, wondering about the watcher when they weren't in search of a charm.

"Roxie?" Leo squeezed her hands, bringing her gaze to meet his. He lowered their coupled hands to waist height, as he smiled uncertainly at her. "Will you marry me?"

A well-spring of love and humility flooded through her at the humble, hopeful expression. "I love you, Leo, but we have so many unanswered questions between us. How could we make it work?"

"I believe if we love each other as much as we do, then we can work it out. It's what I told Mitch. If you really love each other, then you'll find a way to compromise, to find a way that makes us both happy." He peered at her and then kissed her. "So what do you say?"

Flashes of memories from long past filled her mind. Scenes of laughing with Leo while licking ice cream cones. Screaming as they rode the water flume. Sweating and joking their way through the deep woods. Dressing up in formals for the junior prom, especially the elegant wrist corsage he'd slipped onto her arm before escorting her to his beat up car. Cheering on their friends who were crowned king and queen, and secretly glad they'd not been chosen. But mostly, the quiet times sitting together reading under a shady tree in his backyard, or playing a game of War with two decks of cards in hers. All the times when their friendship transcended every other relationship as far as closeness except with her sisters.

She slipped her arms around his neck and linked her fingers together. "I say…" She smiled into his eyes, noting the dawning realization of her answer before she voiced it. "Yes, a million times yes."

"Roxie, my love…"

Fairy lights twinkled among the trees in the backyard, vying for attention with the blazing fire pit in the conversation corner. The Rat Pack crooned over the loudspeaker, inviting dancers out onto the paved pathways winding through the yard. Leo couldn't resist any longer. Spotting his fiancé laughing with Paulette by the garden shed, he crossed the withering grass to stand beside her as she gestured wildly with one hand, a drink in danger of sloshing over the side in the other.

"Sorry to interrupt, ladies, but…" He held out a hand to Roxie. "Dance with me?"

Roxie's merry gaze lit upon him, buoying him with her love. She handed Paulette her pilsner glass and turned unhesitatingly to accept his hand. "Let's go."

"Sure, I'll just wait here." Paulette's laughing remarks floated on the air behind him as he led Roxie to a clear intersection of paving stones.

Pulling her into his arms, he guided them in a small circle to the seductive crooning of Fred Astaire. The lyrics spoke of deep, abiding love, the kind he held within his embrace. The adoration reflected in Roxie's eyes filled him with pride and hope for their future together. A feeling he'd relinquished years ago when they'd gone their separate ways. The present situation had far exceeded his boyish dreams. The woman in his arms occupied his mind as well as his heart. He owed his happiness to her. Owed his life to her. Owed his love to her.

"You've started something." Roxie motioned with a tilt of her head to where Mitch led Beth to an open spot on the path.

The couple seemed more tightly meshed than before the disagreement. Mitch's head bent over Beth's upturned smiling face. Gazes locked on each other as if only the two of them existed in all the world. He held her possessively, their thighs touching as they swayed to the music. He and the other guys had done the right thing by intervening. Mitch and Beth belonged together. Learning how to find common ground would become second nature over time.

Max strode up with Meredith on his arm, eyes sparkling with suppressed laughter. "Hey, Leo, in case I forgot to say it, good work not only helping Mitch but arranging to become my newest brother-in-law."

With a glance at Roxie, Leo stopped dancing and faced Max and Meredith. "Thanks. I hadn't anticipated asking today, but the moment felt right."

"Not unusual." Max cast a look at his wife and then back to Leo. "You'll get used to it."

Leo nodded and then froze. As he'd glanced between Max and Meredith, he caught a subtle signal pass between Meredith and Roxie. His brows tugged down over his eyes as he rested his gaze on Roxie for several seconds. She blinked at him with a slight innocent smile on her lips.

Leo aimed his puzzled eyes at Max. He'd been married into this family for the longest of them all. His insights may prove useful. "Used to what exactly?"

Max chuckled and patted Meredith's hand on his arm. "How things always seem to work out. Like today. Mitch and you both quickly realized the value of your women and rightly claimed them for yourselves. Good for you. And the girls."

Leo smiled and nodded and then stilled. Good for the girls. Did everything result in what they ultimately desired? Were they using their magic to influence or direct the actions of others? Peggy Golden manipulated his and Roxie's actions through the powerful quest spell, forcing them to seek out hidden clues together whether they wanted to or not. At Peggy's whim. Roxie had suggested to the coach he should let her explore the dugout against his preferences. Invoking magic to influence his actions. She'd been sitting outside the Hideaway in plain sight of the five men's discussion. A chill spread slowly from the pit of his stomach outward to his fingertips. Surely she hadn't plied her magic on Mitch. Or him.

He trusted her to do what was right. She was known for her honesty and integrity. He shook himself for having doubts about the love of his life. She wouldn't do anything she didn't believe in. She didn't need to since he already loved her with his whole heart and soul. Relief draped over his shoulders, comforting and calming. He overreacted to the suggestion, the inference Max had made. He clued back into the conversation which had continued during his startled musings.

"So tomorrow we need to go to the headquarters and see what we can find out." Roxie swiped a hand through her hair to pull it back from her face. "If they'll let us in. I'm not a member."

"Your mom was though." Meredith extracted herself from Max's embrace to step closer to Roxie. "Tell me why you never joined. I'm curious."

Roxie half-shrugged as she quirked her mouth to one side. "Mom always told me I didn't need to go through the initiation until the time was right. If ever."

Leo pursed his lips briefly and then regarded Roxie. "Dad said the same to me, as if I ever wanted to be in the Order. Such a stuffy bunch."

"Being a bookish sort, I don't mind their love of all things related to language and writing." Roxie smiled at him, her gentle humor soothing his ruffled emotions. "I'm just not much of a joiner, you know?"

"Well, we need to go find a charm somewhere on the property." Leo brushed aside his doubts as he sidled closer to Roxie, slipping an arm around her waist. "Tomorrow afternoon?"

"If all goes as planned, sure." Roxie snuggled into the embrace as she scanned the family gathered for a celebratory pizza party. "I'm not sure, but I think we may be looking for a pen or something similar."

"Taking up poetry now?" Paulette joined the group, catching the tail end of Roxie's comment.

Chuckling, Roxie shook her head. "The next charm. I think the clue referred to a writing implement, to use for 'clear and open' communication."

"Makes sense to me." Zak draped an arm around Paulette's shoulders as the small group grew as Grant and Tara also joined in. "You may need to work a little magic on the guardians in order for them to let you in to look around, Roxie."

"I hope not, Zak." Roxie's eyes clouded as she shook her head slowly side to side. "I'd rather they do so willingly. It's more honest."

Leo contemplated the worried expression settling onto Roxie's features. She'd employed her special gift to achieve her ends in the past. Had she done so to persuade Mitch to make up with Beth? Or, worse, had she used those powers to force him to propose even though they both knew they had much to work out before they could possibly have a future together?

He didn't want to believe her capable of such a deception. But he'd fallen to the temptation. Why not her? If she wanted something badly enough…anything might prove possible.

Chapter Fourteen

$\mathcal{A}$ nger proved easier to hide behind than fear. Leo tossed and turned the night through, replaying the events of the previous day. He firmly believed in the truth of the arguments presented to Mitch to convince him of mending the bond between him and Beth. Those arguments appeared to have worked. But what if… Doubt plagued him the longer he tossed and turned, sleepless in the queen-size bed, the quilt squashed at the foot of the mattress.

Knowing Roxie slept in the next room did nothing to ease his distress. So close and so loving. Yet how honest had she been about her actions? Could she have unknowingly evoked her powers to persuade, thus manipulating Leo into proposing? Into staying in Roseville despite his intentions to go back to Atlanta as soon as possible? Perhaps it had been her influence which made him feel connected to a place he'd denied even living in up until a week ago.

A shaft of sunlight flared through the slatted blinds, softly illuminating the bed and reflecting in the mirror over the triple-dresser. The room seemed to glow in the early dawn light. High time he stopped stewing and stirred his stumps to start his day. He needed answers. But first he needed coffee.

Ten minutes later he padded on bare feet into the kitchen, the cool linoleum helping to wake him even more. He started coffee brewing and then opened the fridge to peek inside at breakfast options. Best to keep busy after such a wakeful night rather than continue to dwell on his worries. Having fended for himself for so long, he knew a thing or two about cooking. He'd whip up something and marshal his thoughts on how to broach his concerns with his fiancé. Whether she'd tricked him or not, the fact remained he asked and she accepted. How long of an engagement they'd have was an open question.

By the time Roxie pushed through the kitchen door wearing jeans shorts and a red tee, he had scrambled eggs and sausage ready on the stove. She looked deliciously sleepy and inviting. He'd like nothing more than to take her to bed. But they had to resolve some questions first. Like his father always said, better to be polite than aggressive when trying to accomplish an objective.

"Morning, sleepyhead." Leo handed her a steaming mug of coffee and smiled as she took it with both hands.

"Thanks." She sipped the hot beverage and smiled at him. "Did you sleep well?"

"Okay. Breakfast?" He swiped a hand at the stove top where the fluffy eggs and sizzling sausage sent delectable aromas into the air. Handing her a plate, he stepped aside so she could ladle eggs and meat onto her plate.

"Toast?" She held the plate in front of her as she glanced at the toaster.

"3, 2, 1…" He pointed at the toaster as two slices of bread popped up. He nabbed one and tossed it onto her plate, waving his fingers to cool them off.

"Perfect timing." She carried her meal to the table and eased onto a chair. "I get the impression something is on your mind."

"You could say that." Of course she could tell he was distracted. Yet another of her gifts. He felt his guard slide into place. Leo sat across from her and picked at his breakfast for a moment before taking a bite, chewing and swallowing, before saying more. "I need to know the truth."

"I always tell the truth, you know that." She bit into her buttered toast and studied him as she chewed slowly.

He nodded twice as he swallowed a gulp of coffee for fortification. "Then answer me one question."

"Shoot." She set her fork down and picked up her mug, cradling it between both hands as she calmly regarded him.

"Did you use your power of persuasion on Mitch yesterday? Or on me?" The words tumbled from his mouth before he could think to couch them differently, soften the accusation simmering under each syllable.

"Why would you even ask such a thing?"

She redirected rather than answering his forthright question. Doubt grew into suspicion. "Like Max said last night, everything happened too quickly and to your advantage."

She arched one brow at him so high he thought it might launch into outer space. "So obviously I must have made it happen, is that what you're saying?"

"It's not like I defend myself against your powers. Not as long as I don't have access to mine, I mean." He gripped his fork so tightly it bent under the pressure. Dropping it to the table, he glared at her. "Which we both know is never going to happen, thanks to your mother."

She huffed in disgust. "You're bringing my mother into this argument about your lack of trust in me?" She leaned against her chair and aimed angry eyes at him, sparks practically shooting from their depths the longer she considered the accusations he'd made. "How dare you?"

"Back at ya, sister. Why did you do it?" He gripped the edge of the table and hoped he didn't splinter the wood. "Just because it worked on Coach didn't mean you should use it on your future brother-in-law or me as your future husband."

"I'd never do such a thing and if you were in your right mind you'd know it." She jumped up from her seat, the chair crashing to the floor behind her. Tears sprang to her eyes and rolled down her cheeks. She rubbed them away with a fist. "I can't even stand to look at you right now."

Roxie spun and marched out of the room, the door slamming shut behind her. Leo heard her footsteps race up the stairs and the distant slam of her bedroom door.

Alone, he stared mutely at the remains of his breakfast. Her barely touched plate. Shoved his plate away from him, appetite gone. A shaft of pain stabbed his heart as he recalled the sorrow and disappointment on Roxie's face before she'd fled his presence. Of course she denied her actions. Denied finagling the outcome she wanted all along, ever since he'd stepped foot in the Golden Owl. He tensed, resisting the sudden inexplicable urge to go after her. To comfort her. She'd wronged both him and Mitch by her underhanded dealings. Indeed, how long had she been influencing him? Probably since he'd arrived in town and they'd unearthed the quest spell. Manipulating him. That's what she'd been doing all along. Every step of the way.

Hadn't she? Of course, she must have been. There wasn't any other possible explanation. Then why did his heart slowly break into jagged fragments in his chest at the thought of the pain he'd inflicted on her with his charges?

The walls closed in on her. Four strides, pause, pivot. Four strides, pause, pivot. Her marching steps reverberated on the wood floor as she strove to dispel the angry energy inside. Resentment and hurt created a vortex of grief in her chest, building into a pain which spread throughout her core.

How could he think she'd coerce him into having feelings for her? How dare he think she wasn't worth his real love without such machinations? They'd loved each other without question once upon a time. Now he thought she needed magic to win him over. She dragged in a deep breath, fighting for calm. Failed. Pivot and stride. A glance out the window at the sunshine falling on the quiet street, a normal afternoon and yet not.

She whirled around and her gaze landed on a framed photo of them goofing around out at the park. Crossing to the dresser, she picked up the silver frame in both hands. Leo held up two fingers behind her as she splayed her arms wide and waggled her fingers to create jazz hands. They both grinned foolishly, enjoying the antics on a bright spring day. Kids. They'd been so young and naive. And in love even if they hadn't realized it at the time.

She set the picture back in place and put her hands on her hips. Studied the smiles and recalled the laughter they'd shared. Where had it gone? More importantly, how could they retrieve it?

"Ugh." Grabbing up her brush, she dragged it through her hair with quick strokes. "He's going to run, if I don't do something."

A few more strokes then she tossed the brush onto the dresser beside the picture. Pulled her hair up into a ponytail and secured it with a hair tie. Stared at herself in the mirror for several seconds. Hiding in her room accomplished nothing. On a huff, she shook her head then strode to the door.

She found him still in the kitchen, sitting at the table with a cooling cup of coffee. "We need to talk."

He looked up at her when she stopped in front of him. His expression guarded and wary. "Can I trust you to not use your power of persuasion with every word you utter?"

"Get over it, Leo. You know me better than that." She flopped onto the chair opposite and reached for his mug, took a swallow. "I'd never need to do that with you. Right?"

"I didn't think so, but you've proven me wrong." He snatched his mug back and held onto it. "Why did you have to do such an underhanded trick?"

He didn't believe her. Didn't trust her. Hurt and disbelief filled her heart. After all they'd been through. All they'd meant to each other. The happy times. The loving times.

"Apparently, no matter what I say you're not going to believe me." She fisted her hands and laid them on the table in full view. "What do I need to do to regain your trust?"

"I don't think you can at this point." He upended the mug into his mouth, gulping down the fluid until it was all gone. Slamming the cup on the table, he wiped his mouth with the back of his hand. "I should go like I've wanted to all along. There's no point in finishing the quest. No point to us."

Ouch. She stared at him, a frown weighing down her forehead. A pulse in her neck throbbed until a headache began to blossom. He'd come back only to say they shouldn't be together. The very concept of never seeing him again after spending so much time with him over the last few days left her feeling adrift, bereft, alone.

"You can't leave me. You know what happened last time you left in anger." She shivered at the memory of the cold freezing her from the inside out to the tips of her fingers and toes. Opening her fist to press one palm to the table top, she searched his eyes. "Please. We must finish."

"Why? Tell me what's in it for me after you showed your true colors to me. You'd do anything to get what you want no matter what happens to anyone else. I didn't realize you were so callous as to not care about my feelings, my dreams. It's all about you, isn't it? You and your sisters, that is."

"No, not at all." Roxie shook her head slowly as she wracked her brain for something to say to change his mind. To help him see the truth. The reality. Since he didn't believe she wasn't manipulating him with her words, her most powerful weapon, she'd have to find another way to prove to him her innocence with regard to influencing his or Mitch's change of heart. "But you've given me an idea of how I can prove it to you. Will you give me a chance to do so?"

He glared at her for a long moment, slowly folding his brawny arms over his broad chest. "If you think you can."

She pulled out her phone from a pocket and speed dialed a number. "Meredith? I'm calling an emergency family conclave."

Chapter Fifteen

The hiss and crackle of flames in the fireplace punctuated the tense pause in the blame game played by Leo before the rest of the family. Roxie perched on the edge of the love seat near the warmth of the fire. The others had scattered among the chairs and sofas huddled together in the center of the room.

"Is it true?" Beth peered at Roxie, eyes wider than normal yet kind.

Roxie shook her head, keeping her fingers linked between her knees rather than folding her arms. Though the urge to defend herself from further attack grew stronger with each passing moment. "I'd never manipulate any of you into doing anything you didn't want to."

Leo stood by the hearth, his back to the fire. A burst of orange and yellow flames backlit his silhouette for an instant. "What about Coach Griffin? You persuaded him to do your bidding. Who else have you…encouraged?"

The coach hadn't needed much of a nudge. Just enough to give them a few minutes to look around so he didn't call security to kick them out. She'd sensed an underlying curiosity as to their intent which she played on to encourage his willingness to grant her request.

"That was different and you know it." She gripped her hands together, feeling her shoulders lift of their own accord as the tension escalated in the room.

"We're not a jury and you're not on trial." Meredith leaned forward in her seat across from Roxie. "We're trying to help you resolve this dispute, that's all."

Leo crossed his arms over his broad chest and frowned at Meredith. "How was the coach different from what you did to me and Mitch?"

Roxie stared at Leo, slowly blinking away the passing seconds with shock and dismay swirling in her heart. "I didn't do anything to you and Mitch. Let's start with that fact."

"How can I know for certain?" Leo dropped his arms to let his fists rest against his strong thighs clad in denim. "My powers are useless and always will be. How can I know?"

By trusting me, she wanted to blurt. Saying the words wouldn't change his mind, wouldn't persuade him to do as she hoped. Perhaps they were doomed to never be together because they couldn't trust each other not to hurt the other again. He didn't trust her. That much remained clear as a bright morning sky. But she was going to fight to make him trust her again if it was the last thing she did.

"I believe you." Zac spoke up from where he sat next to Paulette on the matching love seat. "You've never lied to us. I can't imagine you'd start over something so important as this."

"Thanks, Zac. I have always told the truth and intend to always do so."

Zac nodded and draped an arm around his wife as he glanced up at Leo's scowl. "You can take that to the bank, my friend."

"But how can you be sure she's not using her abilities to manipulate your responses without your knowledge?" Leo splayed his hands to indicate his sincere doubt as to her motivations. "I know I fell victim to the allure of using my own power of mind control to get my way. It's a sweet Siren, let me tell you. Taken to the extreme, we'd never detect a difference. She's a powerful witch, after all."

Grant leaned against the back of the love seat Roxie occupied to pin his gaze on Leo. "We know she wouldn't because she said so. We trust her. Why don't you?"

It came to her then. The reason why Leo doubted so strongly stemmed from his own insecurity. His own doubts as to what he might do in the same circumstances. After he'd used his own controlling power on the coach all those years ago, why wouldn't he fear she might succumb to the same temptation?

"Beth, would you do Leo a favor?"

Beth arched one brow and nodded. "Like what?"

Roxie had never asked her sisters to use their powers on her and wasn't sure what the experience would entail. But she could only think of one way to reassure Leo. To bring him back to trusting and then loving her again. She couldn't give up on him. Not after he came back to her.

She dragged in a calming breath and then let it out slowly. She grimaced at Beth and then nodded once. "I want you to search my mind with your psychic powers and tell Leo what you find. Tell everyone. I won't have secrets or doubts within our family."

"Are you sure?" Beth rose from her seat and sauntered toward Roxie, one foot after another, concern etched on her features. "I've never read your mind before."

"It's the only way." Roxie chewed on her lower lip for an instant and then pressed her lips together. She gave Beth a nod, not trusting herself to not take back her request. It seemed an invasion of her deepest thoughts and feelings and she wasn't sure how she'd react to what Beth discovered.

Her sister reached her side, laid a hand on her shoulder and closed her eyes. She held still for several seconds and then shared what she sensed in a near whisper. "You've been struggling to deny the hurt of Leo's doubt in you. You're angry and defensive but not lying about your actions. You did bolster the coach's curiosity so he'd want to know what you discovered, so he'd let you explore. Nothing more than that."

"What about Mitch?" Leo cut in with his urgent question. "Did she make him change his mind about getting married?"

Beth opened her eyes to glare at him for a moment and then closed her eyes again, concentrating on the revelations transmitted through her hand touching Roxie's shoulder. "I can see you guys chatting at the restaurant. Roxie watching from outside. But she had nothing to do with his change of heart. There's no trace of anything linked between her and any of you guys for that matter."

"And me? What about me?" Leo took an involuntary step forward and then froze in place.

Roxie couldn't watch the distrust any longer. She closed her own eyes and waited for Beth's revelation. Hoped she'd concur with Roxie's statement and the whole nightmare could go away.

Beth remained silent for several agonizing seconds. "Leo, you have nothing to worry about. Roxie did not manipulate you in any way."

Relief sprung Roxie's eyes open and she glanced at Leo's face. The play of emotions—surprise, relief, trust—flying across his features made her smile. He aimed his happy eyes at her and then hurried to her side.

"Roxie, please forgive me for doubting." He searched her expression, his gaze finally meeting hers with hope and fear combined. "I'm an idiot, I know. But I had to know what we have is real. Can you forgive my stupidity in not trusting you?"

"You hurt my feelings." She slowly shook her head at him, watching the hope dim. "How can I trust you won't think time and again I've done something to make you agree or to bend to my will?"

He opened his mouth to reply and left it hanging open as he stared at her for several moments. "You have my word. I shouldn't have ever questioned your honesty and integrity. I'm humbly sorry for doing so. I won't ever accuse you of trying to manipulate me or anyone ever again."

Wanting to make him stew for a few more minutes, she studied him with a frown forced onto her face. He seemed desperate to prove himself to her but she held him at bay as she studied him, her gaze flitting from eyes to mouth to shoulders and back to meet his concerned look.

"If you're truly repentant, then there's one thing you must do to prove to me and everyone gathered here of your remorse and promise for our future." She folded her arms over her chest and stared at him, striving to keep the smile from emerging onto her lips the longer she watched him squirm under her regard.

The man before her may not be perfect. He had his doubts, obviously, but he also had proven himself capable of loving her despite her unique abilities. If he had his, their combined talents and power would be formidable indeed. But even without them, they were better together and stronger than alone. Despite everything he'd said and done, she loved him and always had. Always would. He was more than her *other* half; he was her *best* half.

"I'll do anything." He inched closer to her and took her hands in his. His gaze burned into hers with such an intensity she could feel the hope and love streaming into her gaze. "Name it."

She lifted her chin and finally allowed the smile to blossom. "Leo King, will you marry me?"

The next morning Roxie sat silently beside her fiancé as they wound their way out into the countryside surrounding

Roseville. The newness of their engagement sat brightly on her shoulders. A shiny thing to be admired with some amount of awe, handle like a pet returned home to be loved and coddled. Glancing at his serene profile, she sensed he felt akin to her pleasure at facing the future together. One last charm to retrieve, hopefully waiting for them at the Order of Witchery Lore's headquarters. Soon they'd know whether the quest was complete or if they had interpreted the riddle incorrectly. Either way, they'd be together. Somehow they'd find a middle ground to explore as a couple.

Leo grunted softly as he blew a puff of air through his nose. "It's been forever since I've stepped foot in this place."

"Same here. I hope they won't mind us poking around." What if they denied them entry? While related to former high-ranking members, neither of them were initiated into the Order. She'd avoided even talking about OWL for the past three years. The pale blue massive building stood alone at the edge of an open field. Single story and as nondescript as they could make it. The gravel parking lot bristled with a variety of cars and trucks. "Drat. Is it a ceremony day?"

Leo turned into the lot, crunching rock beneath the tires of his car. "Looks like some kind of special day. I don't recall this many vehicles on an average week day."

So much for stealth or subtlety. Clutching her bag, she opened the car door and stepped onto the gravel in her favorite Greek-style sandals. Her ankle twisted, rocks digging into her toes. She clutched the roof of the car to regain her balance and wiggle her foot to ease the discomfort as Leo came around behind the car.

"You okay?" He wore a concerned frown as he scanned her lower half. "Can you walk?"

She slipped the strap of the cross-body bag over her head. "Let's go."

They crossed the parking lot toward the white single door at the front of the building. Deceptive in appearance, the headquarters made no bid for attention. No sign out front announced the purpose of the lone structure in the middle of nowhere. Leo reached the door first and dragged it open, waiting until Roxie had passed inside. As the door closed and her eyes adjusted, the familiarity of the place awoke long suppressed memories.

The lavishly furnished entryway with its rich azure carpet stretched away from where they hesitated. Gleaming cherry wood tables flanked the entrance, holding sparkling vases of shooting stars and gold dust gently sifting over the glowing points. Gold wallpaper with white and cobalt swirls decorated the walls. Roxie stared at the unusual display for several beats before peering at Leo.

"Must be a special ceremony to warrant such an elaborate show." He shrugged but his shoulders moved tensely. A slight frown marred his handsome features. He glanced from her to the deeper interior of the building and then back.

"It's quiet for so many cars outside." Roxie took hold of Leo's hand, grateful for the gentle squeeze of reassurance he answered with. Unnerved by the silence coupled with the feeling of expectation and excitement seeping from the very walls, she straightened her back and firmed her lips. "I have a feeling Mom would have hidden it someplace special. So the archives are out."

Leo squinted as he looked around and then stared at the double doors at the far end of the entryway. A soft glow peeked from beneath the doors. "The Grand Hall?"

The heart and soul of the Order beat within the immense ceremonial room in the center of the building. Reserved for the most solemn of occasions, it remained off limits to daily activity. Only the Supremes held the keys—both physical and magical—to open the massive locking mechanism. If the final charm lay behind those walls, then they'd have quite a challenge to reach it.

"Probably." She peered at him and grimaced. "How do we get in?"

"We could go find the janitor and ask him to let us in for a minute to look around." Leo tossed her earlier suggestion back at her with a wry grin. "Think it would work?"

She chuckled briefly as she stared at the ornately carved doors. Sigils and signs graced the mahogany wood, some inscribed in black, some in gold, and others in maroon. The overall impression was one of mystery and elegance. "No, I doubt anyone will willingly let us in. Maybe I can use a bit of magic to open it."

Leo pivoted his head to stare open-mouthed at her. "Really?"

She shrugged lightly as she faced the door, recalling her mother's advice years before. "Mom always said to work with what is inside me and I could summon powerful magic of my own. I never really gave it much thought since I rarely need to use much. But why not try?"

"The worst that can happen is nothing." Leo motioned toward the locked door. "Go for it."

Pushing aside the sense of alarm at the audacity of her intent, Roxie strolled to stand outside the door. She closed her eyes and held her hands out, palms facing the door. Channeled her desire to enter the protected and private realm without malicious intent. With heartfelt curiosity and hope. Her hands tingled, warmed, pushed her innermost magic toward the barrier. A rubbing sound followed by a slight gasp from Leo made her open her eyes. The door slowly swung open, shedding golden light onto the deep blue carpet at her feet.

"It worked." She wanted to clap with glee. She'd never tried to use her powers within the Order. "Let's see if we can find the charm before anyone finds us."

She hurried through the door into the brighter light of the Grand Hall. As her eyes grew used to the glow, she slowly became aware they were not alone.

"Leo…" She made a small motion with her hand to indicate for him to look around but he'd already spotted the same group of people standing at the edges of the central specially crafted carpet. The symbols on the surface of the dark red carpet could morph as needed for the ceremonial rituals performed in the room. Stars and crescent moons slowly gyrated in a weaving circle, sprinklings of star dust scattering among the brighter celestial beings. "We should go—"

The cloaked figure she'd seen in the town square mere days before separated himself from the ring of others, seemingly floating to stand before her and Leo. Slowly, he grabbed hold of the smoky gray hood with both hands and lowered it to drop to his shoulders behind him. "No, please. We've been waiting for you both."

Roxie scanned the crowd on the edges of the room. Retuned a nod to the woman she'd seen at the amusement park. Then the man at the park porch. The noisy couple from the Magnus theater. The young school worker. Many other members all smiling somberly, waiting for some special signal or event to transpire. Each with their specially designed indigo owl pinky ring glowing in the shadows of the room.

"You have?" Roxie brought her errant gaze back to the elder as a chill wriggled down her spine. "Why?"

"You've come for the final charm, have you not, Roxanna?" The elder bestowed an enigmatic smile in her direction.

"How did you know?" Leo shifted to firm his stance beside Roxie, a defensive move aimed at protecting her as best he could. "We didn't know until yesterday."

"We know many things." The elder smiled at Leo. "I'm very pleased to see you here, Leo King. It is time."

Time? For what? She didn't like the enigmatic look the elder aimed at them. Roxie wanted nothing more than to grab the bit of jewelry and make their departure. "We don't want to interrupt whatever ceremony you're about to perform."

"We have been waiting patiently for years for the two of you. The charm you seek is waiting for you both, my child, on the pedestal." He motioned to the center of the carpet where a slender pedestal slowly materialized, holding a thick crimson velvet cushion. Something gold sparkled in the flickering light from the many torches mounted around the room. "Please, finish your quest."

The atmosphere in the room electrified with his words. Tension hummed beneath her feet, vibrating up her legs into her core until it made her quiver inside. She gripped Leo's hand and walked cautiously toward the pedestal. Aware of the dozens of pairs of eyes following each step they took, she strove to remain calm in the face of the mounting anticipation in the hall. Halting beside the pedestal, she shot a glance at Leo. Saw the tension in his expression as he stared at the tiny gold feather charm nestled on the cushion.

"A quill. Naturally." She lifted the charm with her free hand to hold it aloft for all to behold. Representing the historic nature of the members' work in the Order of Witchery Lore. Capturing the spells and incantations as well as the reasons and uses for each. Documenting them to be passed down to future generations of witches. "The Order's preferred writing implement."

"Shall I?" Leo held out a flat palm.

Roxie laid the quill on his hand and then held out her wrist. He quickly brought the charm close to the bracelet and the final charm attached itself to a link. Then he dropped his hand away as the jewelry warmed and glowed brighter and brighter.

"Read the spell, my dear." The elder nodded solemnly, his eyes glowing much like the bracelet. "Your destinies await."

Steeling herself for the unexpected, Roxie lifted the square of gold paper the charm had been resting upon. Unfolding it slowly, carefully, she cast a glance around the room at the other OWL members silently watching, somber expressions barely concealing their growing anticipation.

"Leo, you ready for this?" She met his intense gaze as he nodded once then sidled closer so they could read the spell together. Her voice emerged stronger and more confident than she felt, contrasting with Leo's lower pitch and hushed tones. Together, the sound merged into one clarion voice echoing in the large otherwise silent chamber.

Lodestone draws to earth,
Wellspring pushes forth.
Secrets all revealed and
Yields a lifelong shield.
Friends who trust and laugh together,
Friends who talk with honesty and forgiveness,
Become the key to a loving future.
Up, down, over, and below.
The future now we ask to know.

As they finished, she sensed Leo stiffen and then jerk. Throwing an alarmed look at him, she stepped away as he flung his head back and his arms wide. He opened his mouth as if to yell or scream, but instead light poured into every orifice until his entire being blazed. The torches dimmed and sputtered, almost guttering out. The bracelet on her arm flared into a blinding light that engulfed them both. Pulling them together until she stood directly in front of Leo. Slowly the light flowing into his rigid frame dimmed and he relaxed his stance, his head falling forward. The torches surged back to life, dancing in the stunned silence following the dimming of the light. Slowly he lifted his eyes to meet hers.

"What happened?" His voice scraped from his throat while his eyes continued to glow as he blinked at her.

"I-I don't know." She inspected him from head to toe, concerned his skin seemed suffused with an inner light. She claimed one of his hands and held on, becoming aware of a subtle and yet definite change about him.

"Your destiny is near." The elder moved closer and indicated for them to look to one side of the immense hall. "Your parents will explain."

With wide eyes, Roxie turned to see what he pointed to. A spectral hologram shimmered into view featuring Supreme Priestess Peggy Golden and Supreme Priest Homer King, smiling as they stood side by side addressing Roxie and Leo in full ceremonial regalia.

Homer tucked his hands into the flowing sleeves of his black robe with gold sigils of the Order appearing magically around the hem and cuffs. "Our children, you have reached the end of the quest we set for you. Congratulations. You're likely wondering what it all means and we're very pleased you've accomplished your mission together."

"By now you've remembered how close you once were before a few missteps and childish errors took you down separate paths." Peggy clasped her hands together in front her scarlet robe decorated in ebony insignia and magical symbols gleaned from ancient tomes. "Now you are rejoined and prepared for your ultimate destiny. The one we've always known you'd find your way to eventually."

Roxie started toward her mother, but was forced to stop by Leo's hand on her arm. She shot him a startled look, only to find his still glowing eyes staring at the hologram shimmering nearby. Focusing on their parents' image instead, she waited for the rest of the message with ill-concealed impatience.

Peggy smiled at Roxie, as if she could actually see her. Could she? Peering at her mother's gentle expression, she spotted laughter lurking in her eyes. Lifting one hand to wave weakly at her, Roxie gasped when her mother waved back. "Mom?"

Peggy regarded her daughter for several silent seconds then nodded. "Yes, my dear. I've been keeping an eye on you."

"I've missed you so much." She wanted nothing more than to run into her mother's arms, grab onto her waist, and hold tight. The flickering of the image convinced her brain of the absurdity of such an action but didn't convince her heart.

"I'm extraordinarily proud of you, Roxanna." Peggy bowed her head slightly, a kind smile gracing her lips. She shifted her gaze to rest on Leo's shocked form. "You as well, Leo."

"Yes, my son. Do not be so surprised we've supervised both of you all these years." Homer nodded briefly with a solemn expression. "We had to be sure before you learned of your true destiny. One you're both ready to assume."

"Wh-what destiny, Father?" Leo slid his hand down Roxie's arm to grab hold of her hand. "What is this all about?"

"You've proven you're both worthy to take over as the Supreme Priest and Supreme Priestess in our stead. You've earned the right to have your powers restored, my son." Homer opened his arms wide, palms facing Roxie and Leo standing close together in the center of the Grand Hall. He held the pose for a long moment, his stern countenance softening into a relaxed and gentle regard. Finally, he gave a nod to the member in the charcoal robe. "Acting Supreme Priest Michel, it is time."

"Very well, sir." Clapping his hands together seven times with a crescendo of sound that rang and echoed in the Hall, the warlock evoked a hazy crimson fog to swirl through the room. Wrapping tendrils of moisture about Roxie and Leo's ankles, drifting upward until the thickening mist obscured everything and everyone in the room. Frantically, staving off a growing sense of isolation and fear, she searched the fog for Leo's features. If not for his hand in hers, stark panic would have consumed her entire heart and soul. She heard heavy breathing nearby and gasped when she realized it was herself. Forcing herself to concentrate on a calming, centering image, she continued to search the shifting mist surrounding them, aware always of Leo's firm grip on her hand.

Shooting stars in silver and gold flashed through the reddish cloud, sparkling and dazzling as they zipped past. She dodged first one way then the other until the room became unbalanced, shifting around her. Giddy and lost in the swirling fog, she panicked when she no longer felt Leo's hand.

"Leo!" She reached out with both hands, searching blindly for her friend, lover, mate.

"Right here." His face emerged from the confusion of the mist, his strong welcome grip on her shoulders as he drew her close to him. He studied her for a second and then kissed her within the privacy afforded by the curtain of crimson. "As long as we're together, we'll be fine. I promise."

She held onto his waist, keeping him close. "I'm glad you're here. So very glad you came back to me."

He kissed her lightly on the lips and then pulled back to smile at her. "I'll never leave you again. Where one goes, both go."

She realized the fog had begun to dissipate since she could see more details of his face. She smiled wider as the gathering of OWL members gradually became more defined until the air had cleared. Leaving only the shooting stars, sparkling clusters of silver and gold, whooshing across the ceiling and descending to buzz the heads of the spectators.

"You've changed." Leo winked at her with a nod at her clothing.

She glanced down to find herself attired in a crimson robe matching her mother's. Then grinned at Leo as she pointed to his new black robe like his father's. "You, too."

"There's one more thing you both need." Homer addressed the couple with a quick bob of his head. "Peggy, if you'll do the honors."

"I'm pleased to bestow the insignia which declares your rule." Peggy made several swooping gestures with her arms, spiraling her hands together in front of her, followed by a lifting and offering motion. The indigo owl rings on the Supremes fingers vanished from the hologram.

Roxie startled when she felt the presence of the pinky ring. Looking down, she fingered the small owl ring with renewed wonder at her mother's power. She lifted her gaze to meet her mother's smile.

"You are now the most powerful witch in the Order, my dear daughter. Leo has proven through his questioning right from wrong, and understanding where he'd made mistakes in the past, that he is ready to serve alongside you. You, Roxie, have defended your honor and the good name of the Order as well as staying true to yourself. Together you've proven to be the rightful leaders of our organization." She folded her arms, tucking her hands into the flowing sleeves of her robe. "Rule with honor and compassion."

"And remember the two of you have always possessed the qualities necessary to be the Supreme Priest and Priestess as well as to have a long and happy marriage." Homer folded his arms and nodded once.

"Marriage? How did you know?" Roxie stared at the shimmering image. "We just got engaged."

"As I said, my dear, I've been keeping an eye on you. Both of you." Peggy smiled as she slowly inclined her head once.

"Your quest has been quite entertaining for us." Homer chuckled deep in his throat. "The charms were our way of reminding you both of what qualities are important for a young couple to possess in order to enjoy a long and loving life together."

"The charms?" Leo glanced at the bracelet adorning Roxie's wrist. "I don't follow."

"Wear the bracelet, my dear daughter, as a daily reminder of what makes you both strong, but also what makes you better together." Peggy bestowed a loving smile on Roxie and then Leo. "Nurture your magic, along with your friendship, trust, forgiveness, honesty, and be sure to talk together about what is important. Your love for one another will be all the stronger as a result. You'll be able to lead in our place."

Roxie fingered the charms as her mother recited the meaning behind each one. A sudden thought made her glance first at Leo and then peer at her mother. "But, Mom, I don't know how to be you. What if I fail?"

"Impossible." Peggy chuckled then held out a hand toward Homer. When he placed his hand in hers, she inclined her head once, acknowledging a silent exchange between them. Lifting her gaze along with her chin, Peggy smiled at Roxie. "As long as you believe in each other, you cannot fail the Order or yourselves. Now it's your turn to lead OWL in its mission. Farewell, my dears."

The hologram image flickered and shimmied. Homer sidled closer to Peggy until they stood shoulder to shoulder, mirroring the position of Roxie and Leo. Holding hands as they smiled tenderly at each other and the image paled into nothing. Roxie blinked several times, hoping to catch one last glimpse of her mother but without success. Would she ever see her mother again, even if only in a hologram? She had the feeling her mother and Leo's father would spend eternity together. She squeezed Leo's hand and he pressed his lips together briefly, sending her a silent agreement mentally to keep their speculation about their parents' relationship to themselves. She found it comforting he'd had the same reaction to what they'd witnessed.

"Supreme Priest Leo King." Michel bowed to Leo, a sweeping gesture leading the other members to follow suit. He straightened and addressed Roxie. "Supreme Priestess Roxanna Golden." He led the crowd into another grand bow and then straightened. "May you both live and rule with wisdom and grace."

The crowd chanted, "All power and grace."

Roxie squeezed Leo's hand and hoped she wouldn't let the Order down. Feeling uneasy and unprepared, she smiled at the chanting members.

Leo tugged on her hand to draw her attention to him. His slight smile, almost a smirk, eased her anguish. "Together we'll figure this out."

"We've come this far, I suppose we may as well keep on going." She shot him a mischievous grin. "Are you with me?"

"Forever and always, Roxie." He pressed a kiss to her lips that sent sparks vying in brilliance to the shooting stars all through her body.

Holding onto his arm, she grinned into his eyes. "That's a deal."

Epilogue

One month later…

Stars twinkled high above in a clear, velvet black sky. It had been a perfect evening despite the angst and minor hiccups of the afternoon. Roxie leaned her head against the back of the chair near the softly snapping fire pit, staring above and recalling every special moment. Aromas of warm chocolate and toasted marshmallow lingered in the air from the decimated s'mores station nearby. Tiny white fairy lights wrapped in the branches of the trees brought the starlight to earth. Voices from her family and the remaining guests talking and laughing mingled with the night sounds. The Golden home glowed at the windows from soft light in all the downstairs rooms. She rolled her head to one side, to peruse the scene and try to imprint it on her memory.

Hanging glass balls holding flickering candles floated beneath the trees, elven lights to play and dance to the music drifting across the backyard. The old garden shed preened beneath its new look featuring cascading bouquets of orange mums, white lilies, and blood-red roses nestled among cattails and greenery. The backdrop to the earlier exchanging of vows and promises to love and honor forever.

She and Beth had each carried a mixed bouquet of the same flowers as they stood with their men, now their husbands. A smile eased onto her lips at the thought. Mrs. Leo King. Roxie Golden King. She lifted her half-filled flute of champagne in a silent toast to herself, then sipped the bubbly. Yes, it had been a very good day.

"I like to see you smile." Leo settled onto the chair beside her, tapped his glass to hers. "Let me in on the secret."

"It's no secret I'm in love with you." Roxie studied her husband and partner for a long moment. His expression relaxed and content for the first time in weeks. "And always will be."

All the planning they'd done together—all of the cousins and their men—culminated in a remarkable and memorable day for everyone. From the moment Beth learned of what had happened at the OWL, she'd thrown away all her plans and invited Roxie and Leo to join forces. To do as Paulette and Meredith had done and have a double wedding. No need to waste money on two shindigs, after all. The old traditions Beth had been clinging to, trying to make fit like Cinderella's stepsisters with her glass slipper, had been ditched. So they'd put their heads together and devised an outdoor wedding and reception suitable to both couples.

Roxie wrote new invitations with Beth's enthusiastic approval and whisked them off to their friends, neighbors, and the OWL members, seemingly appearing overnight in mailboxes all across the county. Given the couples' love of the outdoors, they decided to have the wedding ceremony in their own backyard with a bonfire-themed reception to follow. New flag stones appeared in front of the shed, which suddenly had a blanket of flowers as decoration. The s'mores station served in place of the tiered cake or the proposed cupcakes compromise, evoking memories of childhood campfires. A basket of rolled snuggle blankets had disappeared as their guests curled up together on oversized cushions to nibble on graham cracker sandwiches oozing hot marshmallows and melting chocolate. After the sun sank below the horizon, Max handed out heart-shaped sparklers while Grant trailed after him with a lighter. The resulting show dazzled and delighted everyone.

"Only a few more of the OWLs are here but I think they're about to say goodbye." Leo settled in his chair, head back, gaze resting on his new brothers- and sisters-in-law standing in small groups with the few remaining guests. "Then it will be time for them to go."

"I'm glad Beth feels comfortable now with the idea of a real honeymoon." She sipped her drink and let the fizz pop on her tongue before swallowing. "Now that our family has expanded to include all of the OWL members, that is."

"She told me she doesn't feel she's abandoning you and Tara knowing you have others to have your backs." He shrugged lightly but kept his attention on the chatting bunch standing yards away. "Why would she worry so?"

"She always has. I think it's because she gets glimpses of the future but not the entirety so she's always worried about the 'what-if's' in life."

Leo rested his glass on the armrest of the chair. "Some gifts come with a price tag, don't they?"

"Ours certainly do. Our new roles come with quite a lot of responsibility, but I think we'll manage." She shifted to study Leo's tired yet happy expression. "Mitch is happier with the idea of taking her away to celebrate their marriage. I'm glad he will have the chance to show her in private the depth of his feelings for her."

"Totally understandable." Keeping his gaze forward, Leo nodded sagely.

"Yet you didn't want to follow his lead?" She knew the reasons, but she wanted to hear him say it. She decided to state the obvious as a prompt. "We're not taking a trip."

He rolled his head sideways to aim his twinkling eyes at her. He raised his glass toward her. "We have each other and that is all we will ever need. No matter where we are, as long as we're together, it's a holiday."

"We still need to work out a few things, but we will." She let her gaze drift away from him to rest on her childhood home and all the memories inside its walls. "I'll miss living here, but I know Beth and Mitch will take care of the old lady."

"We won't be far away at my place. Or rather, our place." He chuckled briefly before shrugging. "We'll make my dad's place over into ours, however you want to redecorate it."

"You may regret those words, Mr. King. I have ideas…" She winked at him with a wicked smirk which quickly sobered. "But I won't do anything you won't agree with. Promise."

"My love, I trust you to look out for both of our interests even while I'm away with the team." He sobered as well, gazing at her with love and truth illuminating his eyes. "After I finish this season, I'm all yours."

"Are you certain you won't regret not playing ball anymore?" She waited with suspense, knowing and yet fearing his response. "I don't want you to resent our marriage."

He raised his chin, his eyes boring into hers as he held his hand out until she put hers within his grasp. "I will always be your husband, your friend, and your partner. Playing a game of baseball is fun, but it's no longer my life. You are."

"I'm still in awe we are sitting here together, man and woman, husband and wife, witch and warlock." She clutched his hand as she slid forward on her chair, leaning toward him. She peered into his eyes, searching for his soul. Finding not only a deep-seated beating love but also pure trust and softly glowing respect. She jingled the bracelet draped around her left wrist. "Would we be here if not for a certain enchanted charm bracelet?"

Leo huffed a laugh, a soft burst of ironic humor. "I suppose we should thank our parents for awakening us to our own destiny. One we couldn't see."

She nodded slowly, a slight smile lifting the corners of her mouth. "One might even say we were 'charmed' despite the obstacles stacked against us."

"Charmed against all odds?" Leo laughed and squeezed her hand, pulling her closer. "Which led us to being together forever."

"Which is where we've always belonged no matter what else happened in our lives." She pressed a long kiss to his sweet lips, the merry sounds of their family and friends surrounding them. After a few seconds, she pulled away and gazed at him with all the love bursting inside of her. "Together."

The End

Thanks so much for reading *Charmed Against All Odds*! I hope you enjoyed Roxie and Leo's story.

To find out about new releases and upcoming appearances, please sign up for my newsletter via my website at www.bettybolte.com. I send out a monthly newsletter with book news to share with my readers, upcoming events and signings, and even a few favorite recipes, puzzles, and other doings!

I'd love to hear from you! Feel free to send me an email at betty@bettybolte.com, find me on Facebook at AuthorBettyBolte, follow me on BookBub, or connect with me on Twitter @BettyBolte.

You can always find an updated list of the titles in this series, as well as all of my other books on my website, at www.bettybolte.com/books/.

Thanks again for reading!

www.ingramcontent.com/pod-product-compliance
Lightning Source LLC
Chambersburg PA
CBHW050301110726
47898CB00007B/2493